FROM REVIEWS OF LENTRICCHIA'S PREVIOUS BOOKS

Praise for *Johnny Critelli* and *The Knifemen*

"Memory is the secret protagonist of these twin novels by Frank Lentricchia where he strips naked the minds and bodies of two men besieged by their remote past. Memory that glows and redeems in one; and memory that stabs and destroys in the other. But always memory trapped in a language so lyrical, vernacular, and violent that it tests the limits of our endurance, and demands that we question our conventions." —Ariel Dorfman

"These novellas announce the emergence of a major voice in contemporary literature." —*Philadelphia Inquirer*

"What they dredge up is somber or funny or lose-your-lunch ugly. The sabotage and sadness are real, and the language out of the streets and kitchens and bedrooms is obscenely authentic." —*Entertainment Weekly*

"Original and lively . . . Frank Lentricchia is that rare thing, a professor of English with writing talent." —Frank Kermode

Praise for *The Edge of Night*

"Electric with ideas and feelings . . . [Lentricchia is] an Italian tenor, pouring his beautiful vulnerability all over the room, and then daring us to pity him, or to call him a wimp for wearing a doublet and tights. He may not have solved the riddle of himself, but he knows how to sing." —*The New Yorker*

"Frank Lentricchia, justly known for his intellect, here plunges into the personal—and dazzles us with a cascade of memories, fantasies, agonies and chuckles. A moving testament of contemporary confusion and hopes."—Stanley Kauffman

"Brutal and uncompromising, brilliant and desperate, this is visionary autobiography on a dare, a fevered exploration of one man's life—intellectual, spiritual, aesthetic, physical—as a man."—Anthony DeCurtis, *Rolling Stone*

Praise for *The Music of the Inferno*

"The novel as a form still lives in our culture because it continues to be the deepest and most rewarding guide to the mystery of people's souls, and this brave and honest novel serves precisely that standard."—Don DeLillo, author of *Underworld*

"This unmetaphorical tour of the underworld plunges into the deep history and foundational crimes of the little city of Utica, New York. It is Lentricchia's most ambitious narrative to date, a confrontation with class and race which also offers the pleasures of magnificent sentences, loathsome objects and events, and grotesque as well as enigmatic characters. *The Music of the Inferno* does the historical novel in a new way, and that is no mean feat."
—Fredric Jameson

"Lentricchia's novel frames the American experience in ways that, for me, were revelatory. It is a brilliant piece of fiction, able to stand shoulder to shoulder with the best writing in America today."—Jay Parini, author of *Benjamin's Crossing*

Lucchesi and The Whale

Post-Contemporary

Interventions

Series Editors

Stanley Fish and

Fredric Jameson

Lucchesi
and The Whale

by Frank Lentricchia

Duke University Press   Durham and London 2001

© 2001 Duke University Press

All rights reserved

Printed in the United States of America

on acid-free paper ∞

Typeset in Officina Serif by Tseng Information Systems, Inc.

Library of Congress Cataloging-in-Publication Data

appear on the last printed page of this book.

This book is for Jody McAuliffe

With very special thanks to
the courageous playwright,
Marlane Meyer

Acknowledgments

Some of my pages were inspired by Salvador Dali's *The Tragic Myth of Millet's Angelus;* several letters of Bertrand Russell and G. E. Moore; Don DeLillo's *White Noise;* Franco Moretti's *Modern Epic;* Ray Monk's biography of Wittgenstein; the Derek Jarman script and film, *Wittgenstein;* and Charles Feidelson's annotated edition of *Moby-Dick.* Portions of this book appeared in the *London Review of Books* (12 November 1998 and 1 April 1999).

And I pray that I may forget
These matters that with myself I too much discuss
Too much explain.
—T.S. Eliot

I

The Nostalgic Man in Crisis

1 · Motion Sickness

A recessed bachelor, living with his parents in the great American heartland, seeing no one but family. He alone, Thomas Lucchesi, the relentless reader and rumored writer among them, would journey beyond his small city's environs, often to distant and remote parts of the country, but only to succor dying friends—chums he'd not seen since college days, who had long since been cultivated by the intimate revelations of his correspondence. At the hour of extremity, he would travel at considerable expense, this man of scant means, to hold the hand of the about-to-be-dead, actually to hold the hand, and deliver words of reassurance so soothing that a palpable unburdening was achieved. "In a most unusual way," he would say, "because of you, I am who I am: because of you, who so inhabit my innermost life." Later, the grateful children of the recently departed, needing to retrieve his miraculous presence, would write to him, enclosing photos of their own children, gifts, and momentoes of the dead parent. He would acknowledge nothing.

When his parents reached their steepest decline, he left without notice upon an open-ended cruise in the South Seas, for the purpose of retracing Herman Melville's early career, in hopes of summoning, from places Melville had touched, that writer's robust tutelary ghost. Then, on a soundless veranda in the Marquesas, while making notes on an advanced draft of his experimental novel, word came of his parents' passing, one after the other, in two weeks' time: *Return. Mother and Father dead.* But he did not return. Six months later, confronted by an enraged sibling, he said: "In this, the matter of our parents, I have only been consistent. The imminent death of a loved one has always caused me to travel." He did not confess that in times of grief-driven transport, and only in such times, was he inspired to write. That writing, for him, was indistinguishable from grief-driven transport—and more than life itself.

2 · Islas Malvinas

"As we grow older," Lucchesi says at sixty, alone, at his desk, "we grow more extremely ourselves. Contact depresses us; conversation debilitates": Words spoken with forced eloquence, like a bad classical actor in an old movie. And yet, except for hiding himself behind collective pronouns, Lucchesi spoke sincerely: Forced eloquence had long since become second nature to him, there in his cramped writing room, where the writing no longer comes, and where he now makes desperate calls at all hours, to contact those he'd barely known in his early school days, and hasn't seen since. Only names now, at the farthest edge of memory; names dragging reluctant images of fresh faces, in black and white, of ten, and twelve, and fourteen year olds.

He wants to call the faces. First, all with the same surname in the town he'd left in his early twenties. Then directory assistance in many distant American cities, even London he calls. In futility, weeping to be told: "Oh, she died two weeks ago. Are you a close friend?" "No such listing, sorry." "I have a listing, sir, for the Federal correctional facility at Leavenworth." "Why should I talk to you? Of all people, you?" "She's dead. Where you been?" "He died." "Years ago, she moved way out West with her third husband. I can't remember the state. I think it might have been Idaho, or South Carolina." "He says to tell you that he's indisposed at the present time on the toilet, and he'll get in touch with you some time next month." "Buzz off, this is Christmas Eve." "She died." "He died." "I died." "You died. You're dead. Sorry."

And it is Christmas Eve. And he thinks of himself as Ebenezer Scrooge, not because Money is All, but because Art is All. He, Thomas Lucchesi, the Scrooge of Art, who hoards himself to writing. He gives so little to others, he gives nothing, who would now reclaim his past with words.

Speaks again: "Lucchesi weeps for Lucchesi. True. Too easily true. But true." [*Takes a note.*] For something more did he weep?

5

For contact purified by nostalgia, for contact without cost, he wept. And for the change of children, the mortality of childhood, he did weep. Pathetic. Such pathetic banalities. [*Takes a note.*] But it was precisely *that,* he thought, that had lent him his tenuous hold on the chain of humanity: His tendency to weep over the banalities that bind: all that treacherous crud that he labored to expunge from his literary voice. [*Expunge: Break the chain.*] He wept that children should grow to become grieving adults. Wept because an abused child was happier than any adult who had not been abused, because he believes that even an abused child, which he'd not been, lives in a magical kingdom, as he does not, as do not all the children of his memory, who had surely grown to become grieving adults. [*Grown: groan.*] Believes death to be the other magical kingdom and adulthood a long transition of exile. In the kingdom of death, the fresh faces will meet again. Until then? If only he could write again.

Recalls her: *Melvina.* The one forcing her way from the far edge of memory to the center. Or was it *Malvina?* His dictionary of personal names gives both spellings. Much prefers the latter, doesn't know why. It'll be *Malvina.* Two spellings, one face: black, stern, starkly attractive, with a long bony body, fierce and flexible on the playgrounds of the eighth grade. At twelve, she, Malvina the dominant, and young Lucchesi had competed for valedictorian of their grammar school and finished in a dead heat. Of course, they'd never spoken. She'd spoken to no one, not even her teachers. Who dared speak with Malvina? Once he followed her home.

Wanted to knock on the door, but didn't. Wanted to be in her stern black place, because he thought it might make him stern and romantic. Elevate him to her plane of aristocracy. Her surname had not survived. [*Good: can't call.*]

Now he has his house of books. He's library-sufficient [*Note*] and, therefore, all-sufficient [*Note*]. He'll build her back, out of his books. Make literary contact with an obscure Princess, for purposes of high discourse on the grave matter of her stern, stern world.

Against that day when maybe the ice would break up and thaw, he'll file his notes in a manila folder. Thinks of Malvina gestating in the folder; thinks of the Falklands War. The Falkland Islands, down at the end of the Argentine coast, 300 miles out where the Atlantic verges on the south polar region, and he's remembering a British TV correspondent stationed in Buenos Aires referring to the islands as the Malvinas. Plural. *Islas Malvinas.* Not since the eighth grade had Lucchesi heard that sound. What is a Malvina? His dictionary of personal names gives him *Melvina,* from Irish, "an armored chief" [*Yes*], derived perhaps from Gaelic *moal-mhin,* "smooth brow" [*Yes*]. But *Malvina* from Scottish was the creation of a poet, who had claimed to discover an ancient Gaelic epic: James Macpherson, oh yes! he knew of Macpherson! eighteenth-century literary fraud, so gripped by the idea of an art rooted in folk culture, in local earth, that he invented it. The scandal of Macpherson's hoax only helped Malvina do what she had long yearned to do: escape from the poem and her creator: leap from the text, leap down into the world, where many in the late eighteenth and early nineteenth centuries named their daughters Malvina. Then she slipped underground. For almost two hundred years nobody named their girlchild Malvina, until she returned, taciturn and mythic, in the imagination of a recessed and frail white boy, in a small town in middle America. Malvina, foundling gift of the literary gods, in temporary residence with a poor black family living at the edge of an Italian-American neighborhood. The old Italians called her: *graziadei*. Local earth; local object of desire; vision. [*Who needs a telephone?*]

The furnace fails in Lucchesi's house; cold air blows through the vents in his writing room. Getting on to midnight. Feels a little better; new writing may be at hand.

Assumes that Islas Malvinas is Spanish. Assumes that these islands were called Malvinas originally, before they became known as the Falklands. But the encyclopedias correct him: it seems that the British, like God, were originally everywhere, and the slow collapse of Empire was like the generous, but wary, withdrawal of God, which permitted being other than His own to exist. The British, the first namers, baptized the islands after one of their Naval commanders. Then the islands were settled by the French who, in the arrogance by which the world would come to know them, refused to make a variant of "Falklands" in their language. The French decided, instead, to express themselves. They *decided:* Lucchesi loves the idea. [*Takes a note.*] Because they needed to think of themselves as the first namers.

And so they called them *Isles Malouines.* And then the belated Spanish, whose *Islas Malvinas* was indeed a Spanish variant on *Isles Malouines.* Spanish ruthlessness was tempered by lack of original genius. [*Brits? French? Spanish? Kindergartners in the Imperialism of Art.*] But what was signified by the French imagination? Malouines? What were *they?* The encyclopedists say that the original settlers were from Saint Malo, and that *Malouines* was "no doubt" (encyclopedists imagine too) the feminine diminutive in Old French of *Malo.* But malo in Lucchesi's dictionary of Old French doesn't exist, though the list of "mal" words is immense.

Lucchesi decides to express himself. Writes: "These islands are small. 'Saint' in old French is figurative for 'inner sanctum.' The Falklands, the inner sanctum of small evils? So I compose; so I would compose myself on my small island, this writing room."

Like Lucchesi, the Malvinas are not arable. They are treeless, and monotonously bleak, except for the millions of penguins which journey up from the neighboring ice world of Antarctica to mate. [*Cold Copulars!*] Mean temperature: 42° Fahrenheit, with winds constant from all directions at twenty miles per hour, periodically sustained at gale force. Lucchesi thinks about the wind chill factor. Lucchesi feels no chill. Rain and snow 200 days per year. Shore line cut deep by fjords. [*Makes a note:*] "Like Norway in the South Atlantic." Makes another note: "Cancel the sentiment. Cancel all sentiment." Cloud-cover virtually perpetual; fog breaking on occasion to reveal, in patched sunlight, herds of sheep passing over brutally graveled roads, grazing unfenced, but marked by their owners with coded dyes: a slash of red, or indigo, over the shoulders, flaring out like blood through the steaming mist. Sheep to humans: 800 to 1, a ratio that pleases Lucchesi greatly. He makes a note of it. Principal import: alcoholic beverages, of course. Lucchesi adds to the fact: "and countless reams of typing paper, so that the humans can fight back against the fucking sheep." Coastal topography: drowned river valleys.

Long ago, East Falkland served as a whaling station, the last before the tall ships, mainly American, in penetrating enterprise rounded Cape Horn and made for the Marquesas, Tahiti, and the rich Japanese cruising grounds: And Lucchesi delights to imagine him there, Melville, of course, ruddiest of writers, strolling in the Malvinas! Strolling beaches of white quartz sand and suddenly seized by impulse, stripping, and plunging out of sight into the frigid surf, to dare the giant kelp coils: Look! Melville's swimming too far out, he's diving too deep! Herman! Don't come up! There! There it is again, the bold bearded head bobbing among the white caps, to stare down blank dramatic sea cliffs, and the vast rolling moors of this awful waste.

In a geographical survey of the saints, he finds it: Saint Malo. Named for a Welsh monk who had fled to Brittany in the sixth century to escape persecution: *Maclou,* which became in modern French, *Malo.* Nothing to do with evil, everything to do with silence and rejection of the world which insisted on taking an interest in the monk. Lucchesi smiles in his cold room. Writes: "Am I not, in a way, more like Christ than I am like Scrooge? Have

I not renounced all for Art? The Scrooge-Christ of Art, who has hoarded his self to Writing the Father. *And* not gained the world. Because who buys his books? *And* lost his soul. Wherein lie all my profits?"

Lucchesi feels very good. No chance he'll weep now. Raises window high to let in a blast of icy air. Inhales deep. The heat had long gone down, and now the electrical power goes too, and he's in the dark, in the House of Books, without a single candle, just as he was about to begin new work at last, the first sentences stirring in his mind. He'll have to write in the mind. In the dark, in his mind: "Writing is taking place." [*Revises:*] "Writing takes the place. In the Malvinas, something fast in the white grass. Arms up. Racing with her arms up, fists clenched, hair whipped back in the wind, a black streak through white grass. Secret, self-contained, solitary: We take the place, Malvina and I."

He'll memorize it. Revise in the mind through the night. Memorize the revision, waiting for dawn. Happy in his unredeemed state. No doubt about it: quite happy.

Time to tear the telephone from the wall.

3 · The Fan Club

Thomas Lucchesi finds himself on the busiest street corner in his hometown, where he sees a woman in the far distance come running, directly at him she comes, with something in her hand. She closes in, pointing something, haggard and middle-aged. He freezes. She collapses at his feet, dead. In her hand, a book of indeterminate authorship. A policeman rushes to the scene, but before he can speak, Lucchesi says, "It's nothing. It's just my wife." The policeman says, "She's nothing?" Lucchesi says, "Correction. *It's* nothing." The policeman says, "Sorry to disturb you, sir." Then pointing to the heap, the policeman says, "What would you like me to do with this?" Lucchesi responds, "Leave it. I might put it in a vase."

A crowd gathers. Among them, two faces familiar to Lucchesi from an old family album: his parents on their honeymoon. Lucchesi says, "I know you." The man extends his hand: "Hello, I'm Thomas Lucchesi." Lucchesi says, "Senior. You're Thomas Lucchesi senior. I'm young Tom, I'm junior." Senior says, "How disgusting." The woman addresses junior: "Are you cracking up, or what?" Senior says, "Your angles are all off, mister." Lucchesi says, "Which angles?" Senior answers, "Don't play dumb, buddy. I'm tired of your antics." Junior says, "Will you please hug me now, please?" The man and the woman hug each other and kiss deeply. Junior says, "No! Me! Me! HUG me! I'm your son." They stare at him. "Goddamn it," he says, "I'm going to be your son." Senior says, "You want *us* to make *you*?" Junior says, "You *will* make me." Senior says, "You're a cocky bastard." The woman adds, "You must be pushing sixty, for God's sake! Are you trying to induce a double suicide?" The man says to his beautiful new wife, "What do you say, Ann? Shall we make him?" Ann points to the dead woman and says, "You get involved with this character, this is where it leads." The dead woman says, "Don't kid yourself. I'm better off." The man says, "What do you say, Ann?" Ann says, "I'm game." Lucchesi senior picks up the book of indeterminate authorship and says, "Before we make you, I need to ask you a question. Did you write this thing?" Junior says, "Don't you like me?" Ann says, "Quick! Let's commit double suicide." The man and the woman eat of the book. They collapse. The policeman rushes back. He says, "Who are these dead people, sir?" Lucchesi replies, "They all throw themselves at my feet. My greatest fans."

4 · A Night at the Opera

When the obscure American novelist, Thomas Lucchesi, checks in at the Alitalia counter, he's told that he's been upgraded to First class, at no extra charge. After he boards, he's presented with a rare edition of the score of *La Bohème*. Flabbergasted, he says to the flight attendant, "Tomorrow evening I'll be at La Scala, to hear this very opera, with Pavarotti himself. The sound of his name alone thrills me." The fetching flight attendant replies, "Not as much as the sound of Lucchesi thrills me, sir." He says, "You've read me?!" She says, "Why not?"

At La Scala, they don't give him the seat that he'd paid through the nose for, but one deep in the orchestra, adjacent to an exit. When he complains, the elegant usher says, "In due course, sir." Minutes before the curtain, depressed, he hears the announcement: "Mr. Lucchesi. Mr. Thomas Lucchesi. Please report backstage immediately." The usher, who has all along been standing at the exit, with an eye trained on the writer, escorts him briskly backstage, saying, as they go: "*Now,* sir, while there is still time!" Lucchesi, surly, says, "Now *what?*" They are met by the artistic director, who tells Lucchesi that Pavarotti is indisposed and that he, Mr. Thomas Lucchesi, will have to step in. "Because you have no choice. All of Milan trembles." The usher says, "See? You should have vocalized when I told you to!" The cast gathers round him. Lucchesi whimpers, "But I'm not a tenor." To which the baritone snorts, "You're not even a singer, you arrogant bastard." Lucchesi responds (*sotto voce*), "I am only a writer." The artistic director says, "Good! The role of Rodolfo is that of a writer. In *Bohème,* Pavarotti sings a writer." Lucchesi says, "I could write a singer, perhaps, but I cannot *sing* a singer. Besides, I'm a baritone. More or less." The disgusted baritone says, "A barreltone? You? Do you have a massive dark understructure?" The soprano adds, hornily, "Do you? Do you have a massive dark understructure? All true barreltones do." The semi-tumescent artistic director says, "Sir! You know this music better than you know your so-called self. Make every effort to breathe naturally and your voice will be buoyed-up as upon a great cushion, your voice will spring as upon a trampoline! Breathe from the very balls of you, sir! We want the bright, the focused, the ringing top. Mr. Lucchesi! Remember nature!"

Then from everywhere he hears the pouring of that warm, familiar ocean of sound, in full flood, and he's laved all over by an intimacy plunged deep, insistent: Lucchesi is beside his so-called self. The Tenor appears: happy, as always. Lucchesi says, "*That was not indisposed, Luciano.*" The baritone says, "You're on a first-name basis with him?" The Tenor, grinning, says, "Thomas, I am bored. Lately, I fear that I have begun to sing a singer singing beautifully." The Tenor hears the soprano whisper, "They're on a first-name basis with each other," and The Tenor replies, "It is always the way when we love an artist. We say Dante. We say Michelangelo. We say Elvis." Startled, Lucchesi says, "*You've* read me too?!" The artistic director, in full tumescence now, trots out front to announce the replacement for The Tenor. The Tenor says, "Why not? The fetching flight attendant and I discuss your books during those long dead hours over the North Atlantic, when the plane seems fixed forever in the sky, and land is hopeless. Then we have you. Only you." From the house a roar, signifying either hope or horror. The Tenor continues, "All of Milan trembles. Over the North Atlantic we do not have enough of you. We love you. But we desire to love you more, if only you would permit it. No, you cannot sing a singer. I agree. Nor can I. I sing. Over the North Atlantic we discuss your subtle disease. My dear Thomas, you write a writing, and this is why the total animality of your style is withheld just enough to rob us of your best. I sing. Write! Let your brain become as dumb and cold as a trout in a remote alpine stream, in mid-winter. Because this is what your brain most desires. Then write! And your passion will fatten and flame on the page and we will scream over the North Atlantic: LuuuuuCCHEsi! LuuuuuuuCCHEsi!"

The writer says, "Luciano! I'm not a tenor!" The soprano says to the baritone, "What's that puddle at his feet?" The baritone says, "The arrogant bastard peed his pants." Lucchesi says, "Luciano! Look! I peed!" The Tenor replies, "Thomas, you pee; before every performance, I puke. Then I jump in and they go crazy." Lucchesi says, "Everyday, before I write, I puke." The Tenor puts his arm around Lucchesi and says, "We are the same. We are exactly the same. Thomas! Jump mindlessly into your own warm ocean and all of Milan will scream."

The usher requests, and is granted, Lucchesi's autograph. The Tenor, grinning again, says, "I need to be replaced." The stage manager leads Thomas Lucchesi, a new tenor, to his mark on the first act set.

Curtain going up.

II

High Blood Pleasure

1 · Birth of an Artist

Thomas Lucchesi at sixteen: at table on Easter, his full-bodied relatives filling the tiny dining room, they're sucking up all the oxygen, when he feels it for the first time: the sensation of flying backwards. His eyes glazed and fixed on the receding scene, he betrays them all, as he sails away from the wine-dark conversation, the flushed faces, the swirling quips of insiders, quipping quips of the inside.

Lucchesi leaves the table on the second floor of this narrow, ill-insulated two-family house, where only the soft-footed and the taciturn may keep their secrets. Goes directly to the small back porch overlooking the garden of his immigrant father's delight, there to stare in solitude, in the quiet beyond the crashing voices, at the house across the way. The house partially obscured by the outsized cherry tree, planted thirty years ago by Thomas Lucchesi senior, looming now over the garden, the neighborhood, the city. He's leaning into the railing, staring at her house.

Once, he'd called her, but hung up just as soon as she said

Hello. They've never spoken; he's too much in love to speak. He prefers to think, scheme, imagine. Now, for example, of creating a path of 8½ by 11 pages of white typing paper. From his back door, through the garden, around the cherry tree, over the fence, into her yard, to her back door. On each piece, drawn in flaming red crayon, a fat bold arrow pulling her initials. All the arrows pointing in the same direction: From her door to his. He smiles a little. Even at sixteen, he's capable (somewhat) of smiling at his passion. And yet, he enjoys it so much, languishes, really, in the thought of his passivity. How he loves the vision! She'll come running over the untrodden white pages. From some terror, she'll come running into his strong arms, drawn irresistibly by his first work of literature.

Remembers something beautiful he'd read in a book. His most enjoyable and useless ideas come from books. An Italian named Calvino had written about a boy who lived in trees, never coming to earth. Doing everything in the trees. Everything. He, Tom junior, could leap from the porch to the cherry tree. It could be done. Walk over the thick limbs that lean into her yard. Lure her up, then make love to her, as the great boughs shake and shudder. Tumescent he stands, staring and resentful.

Runs fingers over his acne; feels the urge to throw rocks; get her attention with rocks. Because, as his playground friends always said: "Tommy, what an arm you got!" Then they'd recount his amazing feat, three summers ago, he, a skinny thirteen year old, the smallest of the players, standing in medium deep center field in a pick-up softball game with a number of big kids, when a fly ball is hit high to him in the bottom of the ninth, his team ahead by one run, the bases loaded, one out, he's backing up a step or two to catch the ball and the big fast kid on third base is tagging up and bolting toward home for the tying run as young Tom rears back gripping the big soft ball almost too big for his hand and fires it—a frozen rope, a rocket all the way home on the fly and the big kid is out by a mile! On the back porch, he's calling back his pleasure, the act of firing his rocket-throw home, the gymnastic follow-through nearly spinning him head over heels, he'd almost left his whirling body behind. Is he remembering? Is this what is called memory? That day three summers ago, he'd whirled out to the edge of himself, but had not succeeded in throwing himself beyond himself. Now, staring through the cherry tree, young Tom crosses the line: he revises the past. Sees himself on the playing field in the follow-through actually cartwheeling and feels launched to a place of ecstatic freedom: whirling on the back porch into the embrace of imagination, and requited love at last.

Certainly, from the porch, he could do it. Fire high, so high the first rock, quickly followed by two others fired less high so that all three missiles could rain down thunder on her roof, one two three. That would get her attention. He conjures a different image: she and her parents sitting complacently, sunning themselves in their backyard, when his terrible swift rocks come raining down upon their heads. The rocks, attached to long, long colorful ribbons, falling from on high with deadly force. He hears the screams. Sees the thick pink particulars of brain-spray. He lingers. The screams. The brain-spray. At the last possible moment, with a flick of his manly wrist, the great Lucchesi jerks the ribbons and deflects the fatal trajectory, and saves her, but not the parents, he, still tumescent and staring, still leaning, this bloody fantacist, so deadfaced in the silence, thinking of himself as the unravished groom of quietness.

That night, in his room, he searches his huge dictionary for a synonym for "quietness." Because "quietness" feels anemic to him. Finds "quietude": so thick with aural substance. That's the one. Some balls in it. *Tude. Dude. Doood.* Strange. A noun was supposed to be a person, place, or thing, they told him at school. This abstract word doesn't qualify, but it feels like a noun nonetheless. Abstract only because it was all at once a person, a place, and a thing. An abstraction oozing nounhood. Yes. *Quietude.* It was what he felt stirring within himself at table, on Easter, then found on the back porch, where he found something better than himself.

Takes his jackknife and descends into the garden. Standing in moonlight under his father's poem, the great cherry tree—no cherry tree had ever been grown so big—he carves into the oozing, the sap-encrusted trunk. He carves in as deeply as he can:

T L, jr.

2 · Upon Completing His First Novel, Lucchesi Dreams of Fatherhood

Big Daddy Snake, Mommy Snake, and little Baby Snake are hard for Writing-Daddy to find. They disappear under rugs and beds and the cushions of couches. They slither into the pasta kettle! Cling to the inner lip of the toilet bowl, unseen, even as Writing-Daddy sits. Here he comes! BIG DADDY SNAKE! Bigger than ever for having swallowed Mommy and Baby, and coming fast for Dreamer Lucchesi (quite a nice-sized Daddy himself) who takes his long-handled shovel and tries and tries and TRIES to chop off Big Daddy's head, to no avail, as the big head spits big all over Daddy Lucchesi, who continues to chop, to no avail. See Writing-Daddy drip venom! Watch Writing-Daddy lick himself yummy! Again, Daddy! Chop Daddy!

3 · On Holiday

I'm in between medical appointments, and Barnes & Noble happens to be located in between. I'm eating a half-sandwich of grilled vegetables, drinking a small bottle of alpine spring water, when he spots me: a clerk, my long-absent next-door neighbor. He says, as he sits, "Tom, may I join you?" I say, "If you must." He says, "You probably noticed that I separated from my wife." I say, "I never noticed." He says, "The bone in her throat was, I rolled over in bed and hit her." I say, "I'm sorry." He says, "It was an accident. You still writing those books?" I say, "I'm in between unpublished books. I'm relaxing." He says, "Oh." I avert my gaze. He says, "To be honest, it's a case of domestic violence. You probably heard her scream." I say, "My ears ring constantly. It's a permanent condition." He says, "I hit her twice in church." I say, "Accidentally?" He says, "I'm a lucky man. My wife loves me." I look down at my plate and say, "So you're working here now." He says, "I'm reading all the books. How come they don't have any of yours?" I look up. He says, "You look tired. Are you sick?" I say, "I was sick. I'm okay now. I'm relaxing." He says, "Did you ever hit your wife?" I say, "As you no doubt recall, I'm not married. Nor have I ever been married." He says, "Don't get snotty with me. I'm bigger than you. I'm bigger." I say, "I'm sorry." He says, "Does your wife love you?" I say, "Yes." He says, "That didn't stop me, did it?" I say, "Why should love have to bear that burden?" My neighbor rises and says, "Before I go, tell me the name of that book you supposedly finished." He extends his hand. From my sitting position, I shake his hand, and say, *The Joy of Writing.*" He says, "Whatever you had, my friend, you're not over it."

4 · Sitdown at the Heartland Hotel

He was probably already starting to die from a brain tumor, he'd be dead in a year, when he came to Heartland City to attend his niece's wedding. Outside his hotel room door, a big man sat, who must have gone 400 pounds, on a burnished chair he sat smoldering, and let Tommy and me in without a word.

In the room, alone: Gaetano Lucchese, most powerful and reticent of the New York Mafia dons, also known as Thomas (Three-Finger Brown) Lucchese, five feet tall and skinny, morosely watching the *Arthur Godfrey Show* and awaiting the appearance of Arthur's special guest, the stunning Phyllis McGuire, lead singer of The McGuire Sisters. Three-Finger in a multi-colored robe, in yellow slippers, his feet barely reaching the floor, and we're in there with him! Tommy Lucchesi, my college pal, and me, the groom-to-be. Lucchese and Lucchesi, together at last, thanks to me, Geoffrey Gilbert, the innocent bystander. My pal was a solid six-footer. Picture him next to Three-Finger, face to face, because eventually you're going to have to.

In the robe and slippers Three-Finger was like a character they called in Shakespearean times a fantastic, more or less a foppish person, who was more or less a homosexual. I doubt that Three-Finger was homosexual, but he was certainly fantastic, a walking hallucination. He had a wife, if that counts for anything. Tommy was an English major who wrote stories full of violence in a poetic style. Three-Finger, who actually did violence, had a dizzy spell watching the Godfrey show. Claimed it was Phyllis McGuire who gave him the spell, though now I conclude that it was the tumor in all likelihood, not Phyllis, who Three-Finger was deeply in love with.

"The eviscerations of friendship."

"The ice-pick of conversation."

"The blood-gouts of time."

A few phrases, that's what I remember of what Tommy read to me from his work, not the plots or characters, if there were any. "The meathook of love." I like that one. Lucchese, Lucchesi.

Tommy knew everything there was to know about Three-Finger Brown, except one big thing. When I told him who my wife-to-be was related to, he said that he had to meet him, that he had always felt related to Three-Finger, that he was confident Lucchese and Lucchesi were indistinguishable, "from the genealogical point of view," that what he called the "blood values" of his writing had a genetic basis, and Three-Finger was none other than his "hidden muse."

By the way, he never said "my stories," it was always "my writing." He said, "In this world, Geoffrey Gilbert, talking falls far beneath writing." The way he generally talked, Tommy sounded like his writing. A little forced.

"The lacerations of family" was another one of his beauties. His parents were crazy for him, so why did he write "the lacerations of family" is what I'd like to ask him, but I never did, because he didn't enjoy being questioned about "my writing." Tommy was unnatural, a fantastic himself.

We approached the meeting with Three-Finger, which Tommy said we should call a "sitdown," exactly the way you'd expect two serious college boys would. We researched the topic. I knew that Three-Finger's nickname had something to do with an old-time baseball player, so I went into that, while Tommy did the library work on Three-Finger's biography. We memorized our stack of 3 by 5 notecards, but it turned out that our knowledge was useless, because Three-Finger gave me a glare when I mentioned Mordecai "Three Finger" Brown, one of the greatest pitchers who ever lived, who was big in Three-Finger's adolescence, I had no interest after the glare in going further into Mordecai's heroic American story and how he turned his handicap into a terrific asset, throwing the meanest sinker in history. As for what Tommy had accumulated: What was he going to do with the fact that Three-Finger had done 32 murders by the time he was 35? Could he bring up the notorious names of Lucky Luciano or Dutch Schultz? Three-Finger, he learned, referred to himself as a "successful Italian dress manufacturer in a tough Jew environment," so how could Tommy bring up Our Thing, or The Commission, or Murder Incorporated? In the end, knowing all we knew and not being able to discuss it, in an impersonal and therefore objective manner with Three-Finger, was like being forced to swallow a nauseating meal and not being able to puke it up. With Three-Finger, we could have no *discourse.*

I thought he hated his nickname because he was self-conscious about the frankly sickening sight that his left hand presented to the public. The fingernails were too long for a man. It wasn't the hand of a dress manufacturer in any environment. It looked like the foot of a vulture, which went well with the severe aquiline beak, the high forehead, the thick white hair brushed back

27

tight. Try to imagine him with that terrible hand in an intimate relationship, which I had to, I had no choice, after he slipped it a couple of times for extended periods under the robe, awaiting as he was the appearance of the stunning Phyllis McGuire, who that pain in the ass Godfrey was holding back until the end of the show.

Three-Finger stood when we came in, said nothing, and then sat down to watch Godfrey. Ten minutes later Tommy sneezed, I said "God bless you," and Three-Finger broke his silence: "Did someone say God?" I said, "I didn't mean anything by it, sir." Three-Finger said, "Did you say sir? What's your deep implication?" I couldn't reply, and we returned to the silence.

Then Godfrey welcomed Julius La Rosa to the show and Three-Finger perked up a little: "What an excellent country this is. An Italian boy with a Jew first name. In my organization, I brought in the Jews and the Irish, even though some of my associates disagreed, including one who said, 'Over my fucking dead body!' Shortly thereafter, this particular party was called home by the Father."

Arthur started talking to Julius and Three-Finger started talking to us. You would think that the Thomas Lucchese/Thomas Lucchesi matter would have been a subject right off the bat. That would be a normal thought. But not a word from the two fantastics. Instead, Three-Finger wanted to know about what he called Tommy's "plans for life," and Tommy replied, "I want to be a writer." To which Three-Finger responded, "I do a little writing in my domain, so I sympathize with what you have to go through. I can't imagine it on a daily basis. The torture must be tremendous. Who do you like as a writer? Who do you idolize?" Then they had more or less the following exchange, starting with my pal:

"John Keats."

"I'm a little hard of hearing."

"John Keats."

"I heard of him, but we never met."

"John (The Lung) Keats."

"The Lung?"

"The Lung."

"They call a writer The Lung?"

"He died of tuberculosis."

"This is not the Keats I was referring to. The Keats I was referring to won't die of tuberculosis because he's a Jew cocksucker."

"As far as I know, Keats the writer sucked no—"

"You getting snotty with me?"

"No, Mr. Lucchese. I was merely indicating that Keats the writer was no doubt a heterosexual, apparently."

A big silence.

Tommy says again, "A heterosexual."

Three-Finger says to me, "He was merely indicating. How often do you merely indicate, Geoffrey Gilbert?"

I say nothing.

Three-Finger says, "An associate of mine once told me that art and sucking cock go hand in hand."

Tommy laughs, Three-Finger doesn't.

Three-Finger says, "Geoffrey Gilbert, why did you have to bring me this? Why do I have to come all the way out here in the middle of nowhere to have my balls broken for my lovely niece's wedding by this?"

Then he looked at Tommy and screamed, "You got a mouse?" To my total amazement, Tommy screamed back, without hesitation, "Yes!" Then Three-Finger got up and walked over to Tommy and leaned over and screamed even louder: "Is it a parakeet? Is your mouse a parakeet?" Tommy screams, "Fucking A!" Julius La Rosa was singing "That's Amore." Three-Finger returned to his chair and started to sob. La Rosa was singing badly, but that wasn't the reason for the sobbing. Three-Finger says, very sadly, "Momo has the mouse I want, and she is a heavenly parakeet, as you will see in a few minutes."

When we left the Heartland Hotel that night, I learned how well Tommy'd done his homework. He explained that in Mafia code "mouse" meant your girlfriend and a "parakeet" was a pretty woman. I said, "So you lied, Tommy. You don't have your mouse either, who is definitely a parakeet." Tommy had a tragic crush on a beautiful girl who lived a few houses away, who never gave him the time of day. I don't believe they exchanged two words, though she knew he had a thing for her, everyone in the neighborhood did. I said, "Why did you lie, Tommy?" He said, "I needed to get close to him." And then he told me the story. Momo was the beast, Sam Giancana, the Chicago mob boss, and the beauty, Phyllis McGuire, was his girlfriend, his "traveling companion," as Tommy put it. And Three-Finger was hopelessly in love from afar. I asked the obvious question: "Why didn't you tell Three-Finger that your love for your parakeet was hopeless? That would have made the bond between you." Tommy answered, "I didn't want that kind of bond. I wanted to see his nature at the edge of action, directed at me, in the same room. I wanted the experience but not the consequences. He pulled back. They always pull back on civilians." I said, "For your writing? As inspiration for the blood-gouts of time?" For a second he didn't know how to take me. Then he answered, "You need to ask? Of all people, you?" I said, "I feared for you. After the Godfrey show ended, I thought you were finished. The aftermath of the Godfrey show was a nightmare I'm still trying to awake from." He said, "I don't appreciate the tone that you just deployed when you said the blood-gouts of time. Do I detect a satiric intention? Geoffrey Gilbert? You cocksucker!" Then we both laughed, but I didn't believe his laugh. A few days later I knew why.

Just before Phyllis came on, Giselle MacKenzie, the cute Canadian redhead, sang "My Funny Valentine." While she was singing the part about you're not good looking by any standard but I love you anyway, Three-Finger looks at Tommy and Tommy doesn't look away. Finally, Phyllis, who glows. Three-Finger says to Phyllis, "Sing 'Sincerely' all by yourself." But Phyllis doesn't sing without her sisters. She just talks to Arthur. Every once in a while Three-Finger would pipe up: "She's so willowy." "She's so willowy." When the show ends, he just says, "Phyllis, I'm dizzy." Then Tommy starts with: "She is the parakeet of parakeets, far above." As if that weren't enough, he adds: "And this, then, is the meathook of love. This is love's meathook, Mr. *Brown*."

Three-Finger walks to the door and opens it. The big man comes in. Three-Finger says, "Tell these boys how much you weigh." The big man says, "547 pounds." Then Three-Finger says in a mocking tone to Tommy, "And this, then, is Frank The Whale." He says, "Frank, there is an undercurrent in this room. There is too much undercurrent coming from this boy." He's pointing at Tommy. He says to Tommy, "Stand up." Tommy stands and Three-Finger walks up to him, as close as possible, kissing distance, and says, "Frank squeezes the shit out of people. Young man, your shit comes from your throat. Frank, would you like to stand on this youngster's throat?" Nobody says anything. Then Three-Finger reaches into Tommy's groin with the left hand that's like a claw. In Italian, it's called *la mano sinistra*. Squeezing just hard enough to paralyze him, saying "You interested in me? You interested?" Tommy's in such pain he can't reply, but what could he have said to those questions? If he were honest, he would say yes. Three-Finger then says to the big man, "Tell him why I hate the nickname they gave me against my wishes." The Whale says, "When he was young, he used the hand as a persuasion device. He turned his handicap into what the boys called an asset. But he hasn't done it in years." Then The Whale takes Tommy's pants down and orders him to bend over, which he does. The Whale says

32

to Tommy, "You think this is a clambake?" Three-Finger from behind, up close, says, "And then I put my asset up their ass and dig around in there for the truth. That's where my nickname came from, boys. Three-Finger Brown." I try to break the ice. I say, "Mr. Lucchese, he's noted for it, his undercurrent. Tommy The Undercurrent." I force a laugh. The Whale laughs. Three-Finger says, "Did you say noted, Mr. Geoffrey Gilbert? Did you use the word noted?" What could I say except, "I'm sorry, sir." Then I realize I said sir. Then I say, "Oh my God." Then I realize I said God. I'm shaking all over. Three-Finger, thank God, laughs. Three-Finger says, "Pull your pants up, because you disgust me. The two of you disgust me."

Two days later I received a letter from my friend:

Dear Geoffrey,

You ask me why I didn't seem humiliated and shattered by what happened. I was, but not by that. It became clear, as we walked to the car, that you have cold feelings for me. In your mind you deride me. It all became clear when I heard you say the blood-gouts of time with that tone. I was deeply hurt. How can we be friends if you don't love my writing? It's over.

I ran into Tommy the day after I received the letter. He cut me dead, and we never spoke again.

III

Writer in Residence

1 · Moral Turpitude 101

In the beginning, the Dean said, "No problem, he's artistic, et-cetera. Forget it, he's tenured," when a student reported to him that Lucchesi had begun the Fall semester by telling his semi-nar in classic American literature, "I'm only here because my fiction is commercially untouchable. Never forget that. Number two: Let's do our best not to assassinate Hawthorne and Melville. Apropos of which, I intend to subject you to repeated and strenu-ous exercise in deep aesthetic immersion." Thereafter, each of his fifty-minute class hours started with an exceedingly slow call of the roll, a kind of chant, followed by a twenty-two minute silence, during which Lucchesi stared at a closed text and mut-tered occasionally, but rhythmically, "I am all the way under. Are you?"

When the Dean was called in by the President, he said, "As friends of the arts, we're not concerned. We have him sur-rounded. In addition, Jan, his humorous public readings bring town to gown." President Jan replied, "Community penetration?" The Dean said, "Yes. And the town, the Italian-Americans who run this crappy town, are pleased to see him gleam at his public readings. He's the Italian-American jewel in our multicultural crown. His *paesanos,* of course, quietly loathe him. The man is unpublishable. He needs us, Jan. We contain multitudes."

But when Lucchesi told his class on Dickinson and Whitman, apropos of nothing, that he'd once worked in a lingerie boutique, and that he'd achieved "celebrity on the mall" for his finely honed skill in the line of the "hand-fitted leotard," the Dean felt forced to call him in. Lucchesi told the Dean to "forget about it," because he'd made it all up, he was merely "trying out" a comic scene in his novel-in-progress and wanted to test the impact of the key phrase. The Dean nodded and said, "Market research." Then the Dean coughed and laughed simultaneously, raunchily, as he spit up "hand-fitted leotard." Lucchesi, still expressionless, told the Dean that artists on the faculty had the same need as traditional scholars: to integrate teaching and research, in order to make the classroom experience "whole again beyond confusion." The Dean said, "Cut the bullshit. I'm going to let this one go, you son of a bitch, because I happen to personally like you."

Finally, late in the semester, in his seminar on *Moby-Dick,* Lucchesi disappeared for three weeks, telling his Chairperson that he thought he was dying. When he returned, he told the class, "I was, and continue to be, terminally sick of myself. Nevertheless, while at home, I managed to bulldoze my way joyfully through a seventh draft of my experimental novel." Then he picked up the fat text of *Moby-Dick,* waved it high overhead, and screamed, "I have no idea what this is. Do you? Answer me! I AM AFRAID! I AM AFRAID OF THIS COCKSUCKER!!" Formal complaints were lodged by campus feminists, gays, and bisexuals, with the enthusiastic endorsement of a new group, which called itself: Numerous Big Straight Males. The Dean told him, "I'm sorry, Thomas, but my back is up against the wall. I'm sorry because you know how I feel. Unfortunately, you deployed a certain word pejoratively. You put yourself outside the sexual epicenter. Because it is equally good to give and to receive. Asshole." Then the Dean giggled. Then the Dean made a large obscene gesture and they both giggled. "From the Christian point of view," Lucchesi said, "it is better to give than to receive. Are you not, sir, a practicing Christian?" Laughing hard, the Dean embraces Lucchesi and says, "I am so sorry, because I just love your artistic orientation."

2 · Advanced Moral Turpitude

I've been tempted by the Succulent Devils of Sloth to write my secrets in public print: the literary disgrace of our time. But I resist by telling them orally, apropos of nothing, just as often as I can, until my secret life becomes a banality of daylight, so boring to me that I feel no temptation to tell it once more, on the page, where I grope happily in the dark. I confess that I have not much enjoyed life outside the page.

My motto: Have no shame. Reach in. Smear it on the wall. According to my mother, this is precisely what I began to do at age two and a half. She tells me the story often. Sometimes in company. After all these years, she's unable to disguise the amazement, the pride. How she came in to check on me in my crib. Saw that I had somehow undone the diaper, with its steaming load, and decorated myself and the white wall alongside the crib with my first fiction. How I'd turned to her, jumping up and down, clapping. How she clapped in response. Is it clear? I prefer to show my shit, then move on.

A word to my students: live like a no-holds-barred autobiography of yourself, hide nothing, so that you'll be freed for serious writing.

My father? He did not clap. He was tired.

Later, age nine or ten. We were poor, but not impoverished. I had a tiny allowance, which I'd mainly saved. Enough to buy my mother a Christmas present. So off I went to Woolworth's, to the counter of pretty kerchiefs, which I strolled by several times, staring, trying to decide which one. When the clerk turned to an adult customer, I pocketed a pretty kerchief. On Christmas morning, my mother was very happy. She believed it to be the first present I'd bought for her. Then I told the truth. She said, "Why?" I said, "Why do they have to make you pay for a present for your Ma?" She said, "They have to make you pay for a present for anybody." I said, "Why should I have to pay for a present for anybody? To make anybody feel happy, why should I have to pay for it?" She said, "Tommy, it's not nice." I said, "It's not nice to make you pay, Ma, for your Ma." My father said, "That's stealing. You're not supposed to steal." Then he cried. My mother's happy face did not change.

Here, at Central, they will not dote upon a Mama's boy. They will not love him. In the hour of my need, my students, like the administrators, showed no concern whatsoever for my terrible Melville troubles. No largesse of spirit was ever displayed. I have asked myself many times, Why? And I answer always with the same words: Because they fear my vulnerability.

· · ·

After his dismissal at Central College had become common campus knowledge, Lucchesi gave the above statement to the student newspaper. After it was published, the President said to the Dean, "I don't believe that we ever did contain him, Bill. I don't believe that we should ever want to contain this type of person, here at Central."

IV

Chasing Melville

Author's Note

In the dark of American readers, I, Lucchesi, assume that you have read, or more likely have heard bespoken, a certain portly tome of prose fiction, which I must not name. I assume that you know that this tome, which you might falsely name, concerns a character who hunts down, in order to murder, a certain whale, which also must not be named, and which you confuse with the name of the yet-to-be named tome. In the absence of these nurturing assumptions, I could not write.

The book in question is not about the man called Ahab. The book in question would prefer not to be about the White Whale. I am loathe to name here either book or White Whale, because their respective names appear to the casual eye as the same name, though they are hardly the same—and yet, for 150 years, in Melville's sad lifetime and long after his death, among normal readers and the professors alike, the names of book and White Whale have been thought to be one and the same; often, by the professors, are written in *public print* as totally the same; without fail by their students, by the journalists, and most grievously by poets and novelists of easy piety, the fraudulently reverent, who take their epigraphs from the book whose title they never get right.

I hesitate to place these nonsimilar names, which I, being of sound mind, do hereby grant to be *somewhat* similar names, on my own actual page correctly before you, in their difference, because it does no good to write the names correctly on the actual page and thereby attempt to place them correctly before you, in their difference, so loathe am I to place this *radical difference* before the casual eye, so tormented am I by Melville's fabled sciatica.

The casual eye is always the majority eye, against which there is *no remedy*.

The majority eye is naturally the culturally fascistic eye, and cannot be remedied.

Melville tried.

Melville, the Fool of Truth.

That you may not have a majority eye, that you may not yet be afflicted by majoritarian cancer (malignancy of choice in the West) I take as my enabling fiction, my bridge over the abyss of writerly despair. I promise to fancy you, as I trust you will promise to fancy me, an aggrieved outcast of the noncasual eye.

Let us then forthwith, and together, suck hard upon the tit of our aggrievement. Then, without further ado, let us put our aggrieved shoulders behind the battering ram of interpretation and begin the chase by saying with one, stalwart voice:

Moby HYPHEN Dick, title of book.

Moby UNHYPHEN Dick, name of the White Whale.

Listen.

The arrogant book is speaking:

"By my title, I refer to myself, a fullness, a work of art, and not to the hyphen-deprived White Whale, quintessence of nothing, which you find in my pages, which I permit to haunt some

very few of my pages, as an element of myself, which you confuse with me. You, who have no care. The White Whale is large;
I am immense."

You must hold it in mind, this atrocity of mine, "unhyphen,"
constantly hold it constantly in the center of your mind and
never think it equivalent, for example, to Moby (space) Dick. In
the event that you should find yourself choking, find yourself
gagging on my atrocity of writing "unhyphen," for instant re-
lief you may think Moby (disconnected from) Dick, a form that
does not beshit, or in any other way dishonor Moby UNHYPHEN
Dick, which uniquely conveys the annihilating truth of something missing, a lack at the core of the real, whereas, *whereas!*

Do not abandon me.

The arrogantly hyphenated title whispers that we are in the
presence of a serious writer, bethinking himself the antithetical God of Art, who would fill the absence at the core of the
First God's faulty creation, the Faulty Creation of the First Father,
filled all brimming with the son's spermatic writing. Melville was
the son who wrote because he had no choice. He believed himself
abandoned; he was a son.

What choice did even I have, who was not abandoned *in the
formal manner?* Am I not a writing son? Of no renown, and fewer
pages?

Moby HYPHEN Dick is to Moby UNHYPHEN Dick as the world is
to a single thing in the world. Think of the biggest single thing
in the world; form an image of it; consider its shape, its location.

Is it not, in truth, small? For is it not, always, *somewhere?* Surrounded, in a context? Then try to envision the world in itself. Not the earth. The world. I beg you not to confuse world with earth. The earth is somewhere. The earth is small. The words "in itself" can not pertain to the world, because the world is *not within itself.*

What? You can not give it shape or location?

What is the word "world" but our doubtful word-barrier against the fatal seepage, the intermittent slow drip into the real, from behind the back of the real, of a palpable but unspeakable vagueness, a "namelessness" which is the goal of the son-writer to confront and overcome with his doubtful words? Shall his sperm fail?

More importantly, shall mine?

That which makes all places possible—the world!—has no place and no shape.

Are you still there?

The world is a spreading amorphous haze, a portent uncapturable, not even by the most vivid of words, and so is Moby HYPHEN Dick, which is nothing less than an abandoned son's (a son's, it is enough to say a son's) final retort to the voids of the Father God, voids flowing from the unbottomed reservoir of His Fatherly Nothingness.

The Father with a capital letter is the false transcendental; apotheosis of the lower case, finitudinous father, who hides in heaven-haven, trying to escape the son's unforgiving gaze.

And the White Whale?

You have an inkling, do you not?

Melville's plunge into the plenitude swallowing voidworld, the monstrous unwanted birth of his own writing, from which no Jonah ever returns. Moby Hyphen Dick; Or The Whale, is not the full, so-called title: it's a statement of alternatives.

Certo! The book in question, whatever it prefers, is about the White Whale.

Think of it, while you still can (the latest biopsy is negative), think of the hyphenate (hereinafter M-D) as The Suicidal Art Myth by and about Herman Melville, son of an immortally problematic father (a father), whose successful business goes into a sudden death dive, followed by the steeper dive of his health. In debt, a public embarrassment—incoherent, obscene, and raving, he dies when Herman is twelve: Herman thus delivered to the mother who was not *up to the job*, whom he cruelly recasts in M-D, even as he recasts himself (less cruelly, of course) as Ishmael in the wilderness, exiled from the father and setting his hand against everyone, and everyone setting hands against him.

Somebody says in the opening words of the book, "Call me Ishmael," because somebody would prefer that we not trivialize his Art Myth by thinking of him as Herman Melville, son of Allan Melville, thereby confusing the Myth with its autobiographical origin. Melville preferred to imagine himself the abandoned son, not the son whose father, not having chosen to die, died nevertheless. His misfortune, the misfortune of Every Son. Preferred to think of his father as the absent father, absent in life (as they all are) as well as in death.

The Absent Father as Every Father.

Alive or dead; attentive or remote; *even when he takes you fishing* he is an absence that knows no conditions, occasionally haunting the son's writing, an intermittent terror, slow, fatal seepage of the Invisible Man. And the mother, the blood mother, is no improvement. In the myth, she is rendered as the Stepmother.

The good, the loving mother?

In the myth, no human can fill the role, but only the natural world (visibility of care) fleetingly experienced in idealizing moods, supportive as no human mother can or wishes to be, this imaginary mother whose Allness we sink into as we cannot sink into the woman who expelled us from her body, insisting upon satisfying her own shitty needs.

A dead father. An emotionally remote mother. Double invisibility of the parental unit. What more liberating circumstance for the artist who can emerge only by rising over his pathetic humanity? And so he seizes his circumstances in diseased desire to be bereft of biological parents, to make himself mythic, *inhuman,* thinking that, in the absence of evidence of divine genesis, he will think of himself as an orphan, because he thinks that the condition of the orphan is the precondition of an outrageous orphic art, a glittering jet of metaphor without end, founded upon a presumed freedom to replace this unhappy world of his birth with self-born, self-delighting, self-affrighting words.

I am a lone rat in a hole; therefore, I write.

Or is it: *I write, therefore I am a lone rat in a hole?*

At twelve, a boy is devastated; fourteen years later, by publishing his first fiction, *Typee,* the emerged artist (in effect) pronounces the boy's devastation lucky, but in his greatest book cannot keep his writing quarantined from the boy's incurable sadness.

Melville's boy appears briefly, toward the beginning, and toward the end (we enter the critical whirlpool), in the guise of Ishmael and Ahab both, M-D's poles of character. Better to speak of Ishmael-Ahab, centered in their bereaved author, who gives almost no biographical background to his so-called characters, no narrative account of interlocking formative experiences, the standard process in novels of character-making. Except for one background fact: the only biographical fact that matters in Melville's universe, we encounter it first, and decisively, in the fourth chapter, when Ishmael recounts a childhood dream. The boy has done something naughty, he can no longer remember what. It was trivial. The stepmother, always whipping him and sending him to bed supperless, sends him off to bed at two in the afternoon, there to remain without reprieve until the following morning. Hours later, he beseeches her to relent. She will not.

No appeal to the father is possible.

Where is the father?

No mention of a father.

The boy falls asleep in sunlight, awakes, or thinks he awakes, "wrapped in outer darkness. . . . Nothing was to be seen, and nothing was to be heard; but a supernatural hand seemed placed in mine. My arm hung over the counterpane, and the nameless, unimaginable, silent form or phantom, to which the hand belonged, seemed closely seated by my bedside . . . I lay there, frozen with the most awful fears, not daring to drag my hand away."

The hand placed in his; the boy reaching out, grasping the mysterious hand, not the other way around. Isn't the father supposed to be the one who holds our hand? Why doesn't he?

The presence is seated closely by his bedside. A comfort? It's supposed to be, if this is the father. We need to say that this is the father, though there is no textual evidence for it, that this is the phantom of the father, come back in the terror of night to bring the son comfort, save him from the stepmother. But the phantom is not comforting.

It will not speak.

It is nameless.

Cannot be called anything, much less father, my father, where are you? though I, like Ishmael, feel it to be the father. To be a son is to know that this presence, palpable and nameless and terrifying, *is* the father.

We sons require no textual evidence.

This familiar phantom, this *specific nothing* known well by the son, is what the son reaches out for in the dark, has always reached out for, in the dark.

In the first chapter, called "Loomings," Ishmael is haunted in a waking reverie by a "grand hooded phantom," the looming of the White Whale.

The looming father.

Do not leap to conclusions: the White Whale is many things because, substantially, the White Whale is a swallower of all things: Ceaselessly collapsing foundation, metaphysics of the sinkhole.

Seventy or so pages later: The introduction of Ahab via one of the ship's owners: "Captain Ahab did not name himself," he says in an importantly absurd response to Ishmael's comment on the "vile" biblical reference of the name. Ahab was named by his "widowed mother, who died when he was only a twelve month old." The mother gone at twelve months, the father before that. Ahab, an orphan without memory of parents, is marked with a vile name, that is to say, *a name,* to remind him that he did not give birth to himself.

Then no more about fathers and sons, Melville would turn away, and forget, and does, until Chapter 128, hundreds of pages later, when Ishmael's ship meets the *Rachel* and her captain, who requests Ahab's help in the search for a whale boat bearing crew from the *Rachel,* dragged off out of sight by the White Whale. Ahab, linear Ahab, refuses to assist in the time-wasting side to side sweep to find the missing crew, which includes Captain Gardiner's twelve-year-old son.

Twelve: Melville's terrible lucky number, who lost his father at twelve. Ahab is said to be orphaned not at one year old, but at twelve months. Captain Gardiner's son; Ishmael; Ahab. Pseudonyms all.

And Gardiner of the *Rachel,* let us call him Gardiner-Rachel, the Father-Mother, the one Melville never had, and what he always wanted. Not a father and a mother, but a mothering father, searching for him, the lost boy.

Just before the fatal chase of the White Whale (a last example) Starbuck, the first mate, trying to convince Ahab to relinquish his monomania, turns the conversation to their respective sons. They form vivid domestic images of them, waking from their naps and being told stories of their wonderful absent fathers, great phantoms of the deep. The fathers see their boys in thrilling anticipation: faces at the window; staring out to the sea which will bring no surcease to desire for father-return.

The last sentence of the book (where does this end?); the crew and the ship have gone down: "It was the devious-cruising *Rachel,* that in her retracing search after her missing children, only found another orphan."

Only, says the rescued orphan.

Ishmael must escape or the story cannot be told. A minor reason for his survival. Ishmael must escape alone, find himself orphaned again in order to affirm himself as writer, who alone can tell the story because his sole and proper subject is the annihilation of collapsing father-foundations. The bereaved boy, without father, is father to the artist who, occasionally, must remember the bereaved boy.

Certo! We are eager, we are pleased to confuse the Myth with its autobiographical origin.

Is this, then, already, the tedious debacle of what they call, in the academy, a reading? Evidence for a critical "position"? A reading of M-D through examples of the father-son relationship? Evidence is so flat, when cited as evidence for a critical point of view. These few, albeit shimmering, patches of text, filtered through twisted Melville's twisted Myth of Art, are not examples of M-D, because there are no "examples" of M-D *as such,* no parts, however shimmering (so many do!) that can stand in for the whole (remote God) which they would represent.

Patches of text, of tremendous text (tremor-inducing), lose their shimmer when discussed. Disgust the living text, more alive than you or me.

M-D is perhaps not a chaos, perhaps.

And if it is?

Would we love it less?

Neither is it (of this I'm certain) an organic system, each of whose shimmering elements, properly read, will express the unity of the system, so that we, armed by such a theory of the book, can thrust the lance of explanation deep into the hump of M-D, through an "example," a so-called metaphor of the whole, penetrate to the book's life-spot, make it spout the black blood of critical triumph.

Death by criticism. I die; M-D survives.

The book is full of superficial discordant meanings, the ones hardest to see, the best ones. It has no underlying, no deep meaning vulnerable to critical desire. Beautiful superficialities of texture need not be digested in critical concepts, only described. Only?! Arguing critically is eating by force of the will to control.

(God release me from the terror of my will to control.)

Melville's is a miraculous, nearly triumphant effort to avoid the dull death of deep meaning, to stay at the thin variegated surface of sensuous life and figurative play, he cherishes that thinness of textual tissue, only domain of the aesthetic impulse, where the life of writing and writer lie. The only thing that counts. Serious writers who say otherwise, that something other than, or in addition to, writing counts, lie in order to make themselves look humane, when in fact they are not humane, they possess *not a shred of humanity,* which is why they are serious writers.

In the space of seven years, Joyce wrote *Ulysses.* In the space of seven years, Melville wrote the equivalent of four books the size of *Ulysses,* one of them being M-D. (In the space of forty-three years, I've published one five-page fiction.) The reasonable explanations for Melville's frenzy of writing pale before the single truth of the serious writer: *He is a lone rat in a hole.* But Melville's hole is cushioned with thousands of pages.

Mine? I need to crawl into Melville's hole.

After the unlettered young writer produces his first book, out of experience and a few books, he awakes to find himself famous, and empty. Discovers the miracle cure, more books! and turns

58

himself into a maniacal reader and writer, an American Auto-didact (an American), composing apace out of his reading in the history of literature and philosophy, the history of painting, travel literature by the ton, whaling literature by the megaton, sleeping (when he slept) on the mattress of the great old folios of Pierre Bayle's *Historical and Critical Dictionary*, the encyclopedia of unbelief. The infidel comes to believe in writing. Only writing.

He'd gone awhaling, despised it and jumped ship. Later, reading about whales and whaling, he thrills his imagination. The reader Melville increasingly layers his books after *Typee* with allusions, quotations, and outright thefts from the library that had become his mind.

The man who had become famous for living among cannibals, discovered that it was life-enhancing to live among books. More: that life, for him, was only there, in literature, which was better than life, and those closest to him would have to pay for what they could only think, being normal, his inhumane turn from them to literary hermitage.

Each time that he finishes a book he dies a little, then he dies a lot. To save himself, he reaches for life in the frenzy of composition. In its frenzy, composition is so composing. And so he finds himself there, in composition, without need of company.

In the writing of M-D, he learned his most valuable lesson: that it was not in his interest to finish, or to write a finishable book, never mind the interest of his family, which believed him to be *totally insane.*

The point of M-D is the solution to the mystery of Melville's apparent change of intention while in the midst of its writing: his need to unleash an extravaganza of prose that would be unreadable in the marketplace of novels. He semi-succeeded, failed to write a "novel," and entered the long depression of his last forty years.

Are you on the verge of departure?

I'm halfway there, I think.

• • •

Overstory.

Understory.

Antistory.

Melville begins M-D by reaching into the familiar territory of his previous fiction: For twenty-two chapters, the first 148 pages of my 724-page edition. Like a hack, the serious writer begins in self-repetition. He needs to write. This time, he'll tell a romantic tale of the South Seas sperm whale fishery.

A story: with a beginning, middle, *and end*.

Again, in M-D, he launches a young man onto the world of the sea in order to explore and unveil, for his cloistered and hungry American and English readers, strange new vistas of culture. There will be adventure. Exotic ways of life will be disclosed, in titillating detail. There will be terror. His hero, innocent but shattered from the start, holds up the mirror to Western corruptions.

Along with the narrative of the hero, and largely in the margins of his earlier books, he had also launched philosophical and satiric reflections on American and European power, the various diseases and death rays of Imperialism and Christianity.

Adventure plus meditation: HM knows how to do this.

Within an acceptable idea of what constitutes a work of fiction, he's writing fiction once more, in M-D, in the travel mode, but after the strong success of *Typee,* his books distend themselves grotesquely in the reflective margins of the story, they become turgid (though not turbid) so much so that story is displaced to the margins and Melville, now married with children and doubtfully self-supporting, cannot support himself on this story-disdaining writing of his, but his love of writing grows, nevertheless, exponentially. He is gravely ill with the disease of literary love no longer in the service of story, but in the service of itself, an ecstasy in language seeking freedom from the death-seeking plot-drive of story: "All plots tend to move deathward. This is the nature of plots. Political plots, terrorist plots, lovers' plots, narrative plots. . . . We edge nearer death every time we plot. It is like a contract that all must sign, the plotters as well as those who are the targets of the plot." Says a contemporary of mine, named DeLillo, who has recently published a certain portly tome of his own.

The plotters die too.

The writer, as writer, cannot survive the narrative closure of his work.

To write again, to achieve self-resurrection.

Between books he is dead in a peculiarly hostile way, as the family around him knows, as Melville's family knew. With a compassion Melville never had, I never married, am childless, somewhat decent, grossly dependent on others (on *you,* for example, whom I do not trust), and far less accomplished in writing.

Melville's writing life, in M-D, declares war on itself.

The culturally acceptable, and economically useful, impulse to write a story encounters the culturally unreadable, economically disastrous, but utterly ravishing impulse to be free of narrative death-drive.

M-D is the site of fatal engagement, where there are no survivors on either side in the struggle to escape novelistic discipline. Melville desires, before Joyce, that the something that his writing is about be the writing itself pouring onto the pages of M-D without structural confinement, inspired by the library of his mind, not for the purpose of erudite display, nor even for the purpose of ennobling his significance by linking it allusively to the significance of texts past, but because he wanted to honor his literary loves, the writers who had ravished him, by releasing his own ravishment of language.

But story interdicts.

Call it the unsuppressible ghost of Aristotle.

On the first page, Ishmael says that he's once more beset by a "damp, drizzily November" of the soul. Finds himself, again, bringing up the rear of every funeral that he meets. (*Finds him-*

self. Doesn't choose?) He's pausing, again, before coffin ware-houses. (Joke?) Feels the urge to do violence to others and him-self, once again. Therefore he'll take the cure he's taken many times before. He'll take to the sea.

The fundamental act of Ishmael, and presumably of M-D, in-sofar as it flows from Ishmael's morbidity, is to thwart all death-ward lurches, and to affirm, once again, insofar as he can choose and be the master of his choice, life over morbidity, rage, and self-destruction.

On the wheel of psychic disease and the remedy of a sea voy-age: Ishmael.

A recurrent remedy?

Get off the wheel, Ishmael.

How?

Write. To write. Without object.

Why?

Make yourself an invulnerable fortress.

By writing? You're crazy.

Insofar. Insofar.

A story, proceeding from the conflicting acts and passions of a character who is also the storyteller, telling more tales than he can perhaps control, telling and suffering story. A voice by turns comic and tragic. Active and passive. Does Melville-Ishmael know what he's doing? Working again, hoping to sink into the work of work (HM and me): This is what we know.

So Ishmael leaves Manhattan for New Bedford, then on to Nantucket, from where, on Christmas Eve, he sails on the *Pequod*, vehicle of the Anti-Christ of Willfulness to Control. In New Bedford, he meets a South Seas cannibal named Queequeg, and in humorous circumstances, of poignant consequence, friendship is formed, all redolent of domestic bliss and tranquility. Life at sea with Queequeg promises to be like the life of true marriage, and the fruit of this marriage is a new Ishmael, let us call him Ishmael-Queequeg: husband, wife, brother, and child. Ishmael, the self-contained family.

Revenge of the orphan.

Am I giving you good meaning?

No more orphan-isolation; the cycle of depressions and violent urges melted away in love. This time the remedy will last.

So goes the dominant story, the overstory of the first twenty-two chapters, a perfection of geniality, making it difficult to believe the dark self-disclosures of the first page: told but not acted before our eyes.

Of or relating to marriage; nuptial; generative; marked by diffusing warmth and good cheer. The genial bed, says John Milton.

We have seen no deeds of Ishmaelean darkness, and never will.

But after page 147, Queequeg largely disappears, to return in symbolic form in the final moments of the book, when his empty coffin, built early in the voyage during a near fatal fever, is thrown up out of the sucking whirlpool of the sinking *Pequod*.

Ishmael's life raft is that coffin. Queequeg's last generative act crosses over from death in order to rebirth the orphan in his isolation, so much the better to give life to the writer.

But I repeat myself.

I contain no multitudes (unlike HM).

M-D is so big.

Starting with chapter 23, Ishmael assumes powers that no first-person, participant narrator can have. A major actor in the overstory of the first twenty-two chapters, from here on he becomes an omniscient narrator who observes (not acts in) another narrative. This new narrative, which was the punctuating under-rhythm, the understory of the first twenty-two chapters, now emerges to displace the initial overstory, to become the new overstory of Ahab's fatal pursuit of the White Whale, and it drives the book against all genial desire to death.

Pursuit of the White Whale eventuates in the closure of narrative. The White Whale is the end of writing and Ahab is his chief lieutenant. By committing himself to the pursuit of plot and character, whether Ishmaelean or Ahabean, by achieving his narrative ends, Melville abandons what is best in himself. He may not write any more sentences in that book.

You need to tell me this?

I have nothing else to say.

Say something else.

I'll say this:

1846: *Typee*

1847: *Omoo*

1849: *Mardi* (bigger than *M-D*).

1850: *Redburn*

1850: *White-Jacket* (White hyphen Jacket).

1851: *M-D*

1852: *Pierre*

In between books, pure orphan-pain.

Ishmael, life-chooser, undone by himself, death-brooder, the violent man who incarnates himself in the guise of Captain Ahab in order to hide Ishmaelean deeds of darkness, who, like Ahab, is quick to look, tries to look, beneath surfaces to feel the "nameless," the inscrutable, the *appalling*. "Appalling" (like "nameless") is a key word in M-D: What makes one pale, as if one had seen a "phantom," another key word:

> "By vast pains we mine into the pyramids; by horrible gropings we come to the central room; with joy we espy the sarcophagus; but we lift the lid—and no body is there!—appallingly vacant as vast is the soul of man."

Said in *Pierre*, not M-D, where both Ahab and the White Whale are said to be "pyramidical." Vast vacancy of the soul is known in M-D, but fought with vast fecundity of literary energy.

"I date my existence from my twenty-fifth year," said HM, the year he came into writerly existence. The man who invented himself as a writer wanted to be a self-fatherer, who would free himself at last, in M-D, from dependence even on readers. Even a serious reader like Ernest Hemingway, who says that's a lot of words about a fish, that's a lot of rhetorical shit about a fish. HM would abandon that which abandons him: character and plot.

There is no pleasure in this for me, telling you the stories of M-D. I am not HM, nor was meant to be, but not HM himself got much pleasure from telling the stories of M-D. Besides, everyone already knows the stories, even those who have not read M-D at least know the big one, know the name Ahab, whose story has escaped the book, which is the point of a great story (*Hamlet, Don Quixote, Faust, The Odyssey*). Story doesn't need the writer's words, *it betrays him* by permitting itself to be told in words other than the writer's, banal words even, like mine, which prove that the story doesn't require great language to make its impact. Aristotle knew this 2300 years ago and concluded that story (which he called plot: the story in its inexorable, death-seeking form) was the soul of literature. That any crude summary of plot would give you the thrill. And he was right. Because isn't this what readers and publishers want? And the type of writer who needs to eat? There is a sense, which I will not pause to explain, in which *story is not writing,* which is why readers and publishers love story, because they do not love linguistic action free from the action of character and plot. (My one idea.) Melville is now world-famous not for his writing but for the story of Ahab, which in numbers of pages constitutes maybe 20 percent of the book. Add in the Ishmael-Queequeg pages and we're up to less than a third of M-D. The other two-thirds is all anti-story: end-free; useless seed; the irresponsible pleasure of the page, answering only to the writer's (and the writer-in-the-reader's) love of the exploding volcano of metaphor:

"In a week or so, I go to New York, to bury myself in a third-story room, and work and slave on my 'Whale' while driving it through the press. *That* is the only way I can finish it now,—I am so pulled hither and thither by circumstances. The calm, the coolness, the silent grass-growing mood in which a man *ought* always to compose,—that, I fear, can seldom be mine. Dollars damn me; and the malicious Devil is forever grinning in upon me,—and I shall at last be worn out and perish. . . . What I feel most moved to write, that is banned,—it will not pay. Yet, altogether write the *other* way I cannot. So the product is a final hash, and all my books are botches."

1. Goes to NYC, city of his birth.
2. To perish by the cause of unfree writing, in the service of a publishing factory.
3. To drive the writing he goes, to be driven.
4. The final chapters of the book. The Chase of the White Whale. The so-called most exciting part. In the cemetery of NYC.
5. The end of a story and his end. (I have nothing else to say.)
6. Not free not to drive the story. (Sickening to state it otherwise: he's free to drive the story.)
7. Needs to eat; pay bills; has a family that needs to eat. Finish the story, Herman.

8. Death by obligations to family.

9. Where is his love of family? The doing for love? Where is mine? Have you forgotten already? I have no family.

10. Cannot write forever to the organic (grass-growing) rhythms of what he composes. (He's gone to NYC!) Grass, which grows slowly, sometimes; sometimes quickly; always imperceptibly.

   What are you doing Herman?

   I'm watching the grass grow.

   Get a grip on yourself.

   (Where has Herman's self gone, when he doesn't have a grip on it?)

11. Grass-growing composition as banned composition, but by whom? Or what? Not as in "banned in Boston," for obscenity.

12. Drive the story! Grass-growing writing will not pay. Banned in part by the culture of capital; in part by himself, who is not free not to give into the culture. (Sickening: he's free to give into the culture.)

13. He is the banner and he is not.

14. He's implicated. Dirty Herman.

15. Can't give in totally either to the culture or to himself. Saving alternatives: not his alternatives.

16. Must bury himself. He must.

17. His books (especially M-D) are necessary botches; confusing mixtures of story and antistory.

18. To die in NYC, by his own hand.

19. The hand that writes, that feels the substance of the page through the penholder and the nib.

20. The reality and presence of God in an external thing.

21. The page, the page is his treacherous God.

22. The Whiteness of the Page.

23. The Whiteness of the Whale.

I feel temporary.

Daddy. Face me and protect me.

Son, the whale has no face.

Son, we whales have no face.

The impulse to antistory breaks out early in M-D, in the meditative moments of the first chapter, when Ishmael speaks of "the undeliverable, nameless perils of the whale." Undeliverable? Not even by God? Antistory is evoked in the underrhythm of the first twenty chapters. Takes over the book as a deferral of death-by-story (1001 nights of antistory) through the countless stratagems of Melville's madness for metaphor. Meditation incarnated in metaphor; speculation playfully spun out by a writer addicted to the analogical habit.

Did Melville have a plan? The book as a whole has a one-of-a-kind, made-up quality, like a homemade recipe. It's just a weird invention (seventy years before *Ulysses* and *The Waste Land*). Story, antistory; rhythm, underrhythm. The book is a whole alright, but a discontinuous whole, whose major sections hold each other close by the forces of their mutual repulsion. All those chapters on cetology and the whaling industry have only superficial connections to the Big Story about the Big Whale. Cetology and whaling simply define the world of M-D—they are Melville's materials, out of which he makes the pointless poetry of his writing.

Nobody knows what "Moby" means. I speculate *mobile* (say it in Italian, please). The White Whale is said to be ubiquitous in time and space, because he's fickle (*la donna è mobilé*), the pure product of a writing disrespectful of rational categories. Fundamentally deceitful.

So: The White Whale is

the Devil;

an indecipherable page of writing;

a dumb brute: just a whale;

intelligently malign;

agent of supernatural intention;

no, the principal itself, not the agent;

seeking no mortal encounter;

fleeing his pursuers;

collection of contradictory rumors;

embodied imagination of the whaling industry;

the food of light;

a snow hill (and when it melts?);

a smoky mountain;

a tomb;

phallic aggressor;

passive beauty;

pastoral ideal: pulled out in buckets, his oil bubbles "like a
    dairy-maid's pail of new milk;"

his wake churns up "milky curds";

(his wake);

breaches out of the sea like a "great shock of wheat;"

he's just a nice portly burgher, smoking his pipe;

he's the grim-reaper, with sickle-shaped jaw;

irreducible physical fact;

an apparition of thought; a ghost;

a book (a ghost!);

a liberal volume;

everything;

God;

the nothing beneath everything;

a thing of countless names;

nameless horror, intrinsically inscrutable;

yet named repeatedly and variously;

named repeatedly and variously because he has no true
    name; no substance; no foundation;

a thing of numerous likenesses, objectively empty;

inside his mouth, "a glistening white membrane, glossy as
    bridal satins;"

dead, blind wall.

Moby unhyphen Dick is Mobile Dick, is undeliverable Dick, trigger of literary gesture: a writing of seemingly inexhaustible mobility. Mobility of writing at the expense of grounded writing, of stable meaning, in a world without ground (my postmodernist banality, not Herman's).

So: The White Whale is

a loss of depth;

a gain of a world of infinite surfaces, captured in verbal

reflections: ultimate superficiality;

end of theology and metaphysics;

beginning of a new kind of literature;

despair of nihilism;

vitality of affirmation;

the vital *yes* of literary passion;

incidentally, the destroyer of the *Pequod* and all her crew

but one. (The mere White Whale of *the story*.)

Antistory comprises the largest ingredient in Melville's homemade brew (try not to call it a novel). It appears both as
essay (nonfiction inside a fiction) and as episodes of the voy-
age, though not as episodes of the Ahab story; as small, self-
contained set pieces of narrative outside the inexorable logic of
plot. "Episodic writing," in the worst sense, is one of Melville's
strongest literary gestures, his way of staving off the inexorable.
For a time.

An example, the deadly territory of "the example," once again:
"A Squeeze of the Hand" (chap. 94), whose overt subject (when
I cite and explain examples I become sad, even nauseous, and
my syntax goes down the toilet), the squeezing of semi-solidified
oil back into liquid form by men sitting around a tub, this scene
is the jumping off point, where Melville dives into his true subject, not labor and its exploitation (an occasional gesture in

M-D, overly valued by political critics), but the fraternalizing force of work exerted on men sitting in a ring on a mild summer morning, squeezing lumps of spermacetti, squeezing hands, into the very milk and sperm of human kindness. Overt subject in M-D (extremely diverse in provenance, says Moretti) is analogically linked to true subject, and true subject is always an idea of moral weight; almost always explicitly interpreted by HM, telling us how to make sense of his metaphors, telling us page after page, so that there is no interpretative work left for readers to do.

Ahab thinks: "O Nature, and O Soul of Man! how far beyond all utterance are your linked analogies!"

He is wrong.

Ahab is always wrong.

Because in M-D (the artwork as a whole, as distinct from its characters) there is *nothing but utterance,* fluent, like a river, of linked analogies, because this is HM's true work of writing, not the "duplicate in mind," the moral idea, but the joy of the analogical leap itself, whereas Ahab, possessed more even than his maker by a vision of the final unutterable beneath all appearances, feels constantly the failure of language: Moby unhyphen Dick, target of his nihilistic obsession. Ahab thinks he knows naked moral idea, however inverted, hidden behind hated nature, which he finds artificial, a "paste board" mask. Unlike his maker, he lacks the "low enjoying power" of sensuous perception: the fuel of all analogical leaping. He is almost always abstract. Empty, joyless Ahab, disdainer of the natural ladder, is a hollow metallic barrel, intimate only with his own hatred, his only beloved.

The episodes contain heterogeneous material: the promise of democracy (dubious); the charisma of hierarchy (permanent); the whaling industry as imperial death machine. The murder of whales (Melville says *murder*), a metaphor of the violence required to sustain the West's civilized life (says Moretti, says DeLillo: Am I capable of citing only Italians?). Melville's vehicles of analogy are encyclopedically various, but I cannot represent Melville's encyclopedia. Cannot even suggest it.

Have not written Moby hyphen Dick.

And neither have you.

The one failure (of writing) in the book is the midnight scene of the crew in revelry, a crew of global ethnic diversity, all speaking like bad stage versions of a New England sailor, circa 1850. HM had no "ear." HM loved the idea of human diversity, but he loved his sentences more, all stamped with his name and tone (of many colors and wide dynamic range). HM's love of diversity is registered there, in His Majesty's great voice, one voice. His characters are thin; Ahab is a Byronic bombastic bore; only HM is interesting, the book's one thick character.

In the essay, the story-dead form of the essay; in hundreds of pages of nonfiction Melville's fluent genius finds its most imaginative form. In the Ishmael-Queequeg pages he plays with geniality, the idea of marriage. In the essay, he finds, at once, himself, his spouse, and their progeny: his freest writing, which is himself, his spouse, his progeny.

Infernal self-containment of the avenging orphan! The self-made orphan.

"Ego non baptizo te in nomine Patris et Fillii et Spiritus Sancti–sed in nomine Diaboli." [HM's Latin is worse than mine.]

Whaling expeditions were long, extending from three to five years. Mainly whales were not sighted; mainly, once sighted, and then chased, they were not captured. Everyday life aboard a nineteenth-century whaler was a long, long tedium, with little to do except watch, wait, clean the ship. All those pages of anti-story not only defer the inevitable, deathward lurch of story, but they fill up dead whaling time, slay the boredom of the actual with imaginative life: epidemic of metaphor.

Antistory: in the underrhythm of Ishmael-Queequeg, a hint of irremediable dark in a place of strong sunlight, when Ishmael wanders into a Whaleman's Chapel (chap. 7), sees the slabs marking the memories of those lost at sea, and thinks: "What bitter blanks in those black-bordered marbles which cover no ashes! What despair in those immovable inscriptions! What deadly voids and unbidden infidelities in the lines that seem to gnaw upon all Faith. . . ."

M-D: a book studded with self-reflective metaphors of itself, small moments which figure the ambition of Melville's art to represent and flaunt itself as art. Here, of a writing ("the lines") which covers and refers to absence; signifying the absent and only the absent.

Much later (chap. 102), in a meditation on a complete (fictitious) whale skeleton, found on a fictitious island, we're given another metaphor for arrogant M-D, also death-intimate, but this time antithetical to the undergirding nihilism. In effect, an artistically self-reflective passage on the meaning of metaphoric action (as opposed to story action), of HM's luxuriant poetic language, expressing its ever-fresh response to what is given, what is unchanging, what lies always beneath, the nothing that is, which spurs him on. Writing again as witness to the void, but an act of affirmation nevertheless, of an art rank with exfoliating vitality (*the work* of HM's art). The mortal yes of metaphor against the metaphysics of nihilism: "The great, white . . . skeleton lay lounging . . . all woven over with vines; every month assuming greener, fresher verdure; but himself a skeleton. Life folded death; Death trellised Life. . . ."

All things are like whales, whose would-be features in common are confoundingly combined. Like a whale, very like a whale, any one thing in the world's body stands in its own enclosed space, in "irregular isolation," so much the better to defy all general methodization (chap. 32). So the raging epidemic of metaphor, spreading to fill the epistemological abyss with playful knowledge. Inscrutability and death as the motives for the antistories of metaphor, which would fill an abyss.

Fill the father-hole.

First sight of the *Pequod:* "you never saw such a rare old

craft," says Ishmael, who then proceeds to "see it" on our be-
half. A ship with an "old fashioned claw-footed look" (like a
piece of furniture with claw feet?); her hull darkened "like a
French grenadier's" [okay: a kind of warrior] "who has alike
fought in Egypt and Siberia" [detail excessive]. "Her venerable
bows looked bearded." Her masts "stood stiffly up like the spines
of the three old kings of Cologne." [Why this reference to the
bones of the Three Magi?] Her decks worn "like the pilgrim-
worshipped flagstone in Canterbury Cathedral where Beckett
bled." The ship inlaid with a "quaintness both of material and device, unmatched by anything except it be Thorkill-Hake's carved
buckler or bedstead." [Pagan Icelandic hero, whose deeds were
carved on his bed.] "She was appareled like any barbaric Ethio-
pian emperor, his neck heavy with pendants of polished ivory."
The *Pequod* in itself is only and always "like" something else.
The thing itself exists, but only to propel HM into an imaginative
space of heterogeneous, analogical texture. What is the so-called
deep relationship of the various likenesses, pagan and Christian,
to one another?

The autodidact ransacks the library of his mind.

He just happens to think of them?

Yes.

For example (*damn* it): The "visible surface of the Sperm
Whale" is "all over obliquely crossed and re-crossed with num-
berless straight marks in thick array, something like those in the
finest Italian line engravings":

Something like?

"Engraved upon the body itself." To the "quick, observant eye"
—the noncasual eye: hypothetically mine and yours;—"those
linear marks . . . afford the ground for far other delineations." To
a certain kind of eye, Melville's, they are "hieroglyphical." Which
in turn causes Melville to remember "old Indian characters chis-
eled on the famous hieroglyphic palisades on the banks of the
Upper Mississippi."

Where will this chain of metaphoric recollection end? How far
behind have we left the actual whale?

Do we care?

The most telling (though of no story) of all the sentences in
M-D? The book's true secret motto, and the engine of HM's art of
antistory is this:

> *"This allusion to the Indian rocks*
> *reminds me of another thing."*

It reminds him.

Anything and everything reminds him.

Analogical writing, in the hands of this infidel, unlike story,
can have no end.

More examples?

To what end?

. . .

There is a cabin boy aboard the *Pequod,* in his early teens, named
Pip. Small, slight, black; from Alabama. Or maybe Connecticut.
Unclear. Parentage also unclear. (Choice, Melvillean unclarity.)

One day this little Pip, a crew member of one of the *Pequod's* three whaling boats, and while his boat is fast to a furious sperm whale, leaps in fear into the water, to be immediately entangled in the harpoon lines. If the precious whale is not cut loose, Pip will die. The whale is cut loose. Stick to the boat, he's told. Jump again and you won't be rescued. We can't afford it. He jumps again, and is left, as the boat, once more fast, is dragged out of sight. Nothing now between a pip squeak in the ocean and the horizon, 360° of nothing but a spec of a head, bobbing in the middle of a shoreless, heartless immensity. Nothing but intolerable loneliness. Eventually, he's picked up, completely insane, to be taken in, a kind of son to Ahab, a kind of father.

•   •   •

It bears down on him.
Story, whether HM likes it or not, is his lot.
He wants to be popular, too. More than he can say.
Have you scheduled another ocular biopsy?
Would you kindly make an appointment for me?

•   •   •

In 1857, thirty-four years before his official death, Herman Melville published his last novel, *The Confidence-Man,* The Confidence hyphen Man, then walked out of the ruined fortress of his love, the always already ruined fortress of his writing, where he wanted to lose his grip and dissolve in an ecstasy of composition.

He came back to the actual, to the ruined family to which, long before, he'd said no. As a grand hooded phantom, he appeared. Melville had finally closed his book, but it was no longer within his power to allow himself to live.

On September 28, 1891, Melville died. The obituary writer for the *New York Times* called him Henry. Another referred to him as Hiram Melville.

In the meanwhile, I, Lucchesi, as of this day, September 28, 1999, do among the living appear—awaiting the millenium.

V

Sex and Wittgenstein

1 · The Wheelbarrow of Flesh

Nine years after his father told him a strange story about the next-door neighbor, Thomas Lucchesi's first fiction, "Love and Marriage," was published in the *Salvador Dali Bulletin*. His humble parents did not know the *Dali Bulletin*, but he was eager for them to see his story, and so he put a copy in their hands. They were horrified. Then came the rage — long, long rage, which gave way, without transition, to forgiveness and reconciliation.

In the offending story, as in life, the husband and wife are named Thomas and Ann Lucchesi, and they are described as peasants "whose severe labors, and the long intimacy they must share with their work tools, cause them to eroticize those tools." Thomas and Ann were especially fond of their "little red wheelbarrow," because it reminded them of their "favorite acrobatic sexual position," and the staff artist of the *Dali Bulletin* had drawn an exceedingly obscene cartoon to illustrate this most central metaphoric image.

The crisis in the story occurs when the first child, a son named

Thomas, is born. Thomas senior and Ann are said to become "uneasy and solitary," and "lost to one another," until they realize that it is the child who makes them so, this child who wants to sleep with them, in the "big bed." "Oh," Thomas junior had written, "they love their child, but they love each other more. Therefore, they must kill this child." In a memorably subtle narrative maneuver, the reader is led to understand that this story is something other than an Oedipal drama, for Thomas senior and Ann equally long to recapture the intensity of their sexual love, and the "murderous instigator" is none other than the mother herself.

And so it comes to pass that the Lucchesis kill young Tommy and load him into the little red wheelbarrow, which together, each gripping a handle, they push out to a fertile field, "all fragrant of black earth," where they dump him, bury him, and then make love, there beside the grave, "in the manner of the wheelbarrow."

Locked in one another's arms, spent and happy once again, more happy than ever, they murmured each to each that their first child would be their last child, and "this deep concord of hearts" aroused them to another vigorous act of love, and then another.

In the wake of such a tale, how was it possible that family harmony could be restored? Junior reminded his parents of what he had said, nine years previous, in the kitchen on that cold, cold day: "The artist is autonomous. He must be autonomous. He

requires freedom from all of his sources, literary and familial."
When his parents responded, gently, that "the family in your
story doesn't remind us at all of us," junior smiled a little conde-
scendingly and said, "That's my point." When they replied, more
gently yet, "But you used our names, Tommy," he cited Wittgenstein on the distinction between the bearer of a name and
the meaning of a name. "The bearer can die; the bearer, when
a person, rather then, say, a chair, does die. But the meaning
may continue in use. We mustn't confound the bearer of a name
with the meaning of a name, because meaning is just how we use
it. My story articulates an original usage of the name Lucchesi,
which you call yours, but which, in my story, is yours no more.
It's mine. It's all mine." They said, "We don't know this Wittgenstein. Plus, we're not dead. We feel hurt and we feel used. You
used our name, as you yourself just said." Reining in his build-
ing impatience, and leaning harder still on Wittgenstein, junior
replied, "The meaning of the name in the game of my story bears
no relation to the meaning of the name in the game of your
lifes. You can't compare chess to baseball. The artistic complex
is totally totally autonomous."

The Lucchesis did not understand their son; they just loved
him. No more questions were asked, though senior would have
liked to know what fiction-writing has to do with chess or baseball, because in his understanding fiction-writing belongs with
games of one on a side, if it was a game, and he does not like
games of one on a side.

Hadn't he once tried the card game of Solitaire? If someone were watching you play Solitaire, and you cheated, that person could say, Hey! You cheated! But if no one was watching, and you cheated (he had cheated just a little) the rules in your mind make you feel bad, because the rules were other people who played the game fair. What, he wonders, are the rules of fiction-writing? He believes it has no rules, like his son, who has no conscience. Can fiction-writing be a game if it has no rules, which it definitely couldn't have if you could write a mean thing like his son wrote, who just made it up as he went along, he did whatever the hell he wanted, so how could it be a game if he's the only one who can play? Does this goddamn Wittgenstein have any idea of what it means to be the father of a writer? His son was a lone wolf, the main fact about junior is that he always liked to play with himself, but he wouldn't say any of these thoughts out loud, not ever, because he cares for his son. Instead, senior said, "You're autonomous!" Then he hugged junior. Then Ann hugged them both. And that was that.

• • •

Nine years earlier: Two men named Thomas Lucchesi sit across from one another in a small kitchen, while the woman named Ann sits reading out of view in the adjacent parlor, but within earshot—in Mission Control, as the two Thomases have agreed to call it. The town is snowbound at 12° Fahrenheit; Mission Control is vocally robust.

The son is saying, "The corners of his mouth are pulled down permanently, like a clown's." The father replies, "Take a look out of the bathroom window and tell me what you see." When junior returns, he says, "What's it doing on his front porch? I've never seen a wheelbarrow that big except on a construction site."

Mission Control: "It's that big goof's anniversary."

Senior, picking up his cue: "Once a year, on a day like today, the big goof brings it out of the cellar, just for one day. You won't see it tomorrow. [*Senior averts his gaze. Forces a cough. Continues with averted gaze.*] One awful day, Tommy, before you were born, in broad daylight Mr. Salvatore puts Leonora in that wheelbarrow, all bundled up in winter clothes and blankets. He ties her in. Possibly she's asleep. It's possible. He's completely in the nude and he's fully aroused. He ties the ropes, that are tied to her, crisscross over his chest. And this is how the police find them in the snow and ice. Pulling her like a horny donkey through the neighborhood."

Mission Control says, "Like a horse." Then Mission Control sings: "Love and marriage, love and marriage, go together like a horse and carriage."

"They arrest him for indecent exposure, and when they can't wake her up they add suspicion of assault. After she comes around, she refuses to press charges. The word was it had to do with the boarder."

"Mr. Salvatore's cousin from Italy? Who's been involved with her ever since he came over?"

Mission Control: "Who told him? Did you tell him, Tom?"

Senior [*with pride*]: "Our son's in graduate school now." The son replies, "Little Frank is half the size of Mr. Salvatore, who could break Little Frank in half if he wanted to."

Mission Control [*staccato: in a monotone*]: "But he does-n't want to. This is the my-ste-ry."

Junior says, "When Mr. Salvatore leaves the house to go to work, she walks with him to the sidewalk, and they embrace. Except their lower torsos never touch. Are you listening, Ma? Mrs. Salvatore stands straight up, but Mr. Salvatore angles his lower body away."

Mission Control [*staccato, monotone*]: "Be-cause no-thing is go-ing on down there. When a per-son an-gles a-way like that no-thing is go-ing on, but they are think-ing a-bout it."

Senior says, "Our son's got a good eye," and the son replies, a little pompously, pointing a pedagogical finger at his father: "A novelist needs an eye for the luminous detail."

Mission Control spices the sauce: "Shall we illuminate him, Tom? Does he know what his father does for me on our anni-versary without fail? Because this secret a novelist can't ever imagine."

Senior [*rising*]: "Ann! Why are you doing this to me?" [*Goes to parlor. Urgent sounds of lowered voices. Sounds of giggling, abruptly cut off. Long silence. Senior returns with a flushed face to kitchen.*]

Junior [*sotto voce*]: "It makes me nervous when she talks and I can't see her."

Senior [*sotto voce*]: "Me too."

"You think I'm deaf in here? [*Pause.*] Come back, Tom."

Senior says, "I believe that he knocked her unconscious, which is why they couldn't wake her up," and the son replies, "I believe that he loved her too much. Did you ever knock Ma unconscious, Dad?"

Mission Control has swallowed the mouse: "He puts me in another world on our anniversary."

Senior says, "I'm not going to answer you. Or her," and the son replies, "Are you too much in love with Ma? [*Senior averts gaze.*] Because how can you be too much in love with Ma? Your face can't measure up to Mr. Salvatore's. You're the happy clown."

Mission Control [*with contempt*]: "That's not love. She's just something in his mind. In the summer, he sits alone on that porch all weekend. Where is she? What is she doing? He's not involved with *her!* He's playing with himself. Tom! Come back. I have to show you a special trick."

"Listen to your mother. I'm not talking. Quit it, Ann."

Junior says, "Mr. Salvatore is very unhappy."

Mission Control: "We want our son to be happy."

Junior says, "Mr. Salvatore is also very happy."

Senior replies, "This is over my head," and the son begins to float away: "Everything that Mr. Salvatore needs is inside himself. Everything. No one can ever live up to his feelings. They're too big. He's deeply grateful to Little Frank for the gift of autonomy."

Senior says, "The gift of what?"

Mission Control [*with anger*]: "If you need to idolize some-body, I recommend your father. Because what goes on next door is selfish. Or is this what a writer likes? Your father doesn't love me too much. He just loves me." [*Junior looks at Senior; Senior looks away.*]

Junior [*staring at the floor*]: "Everything he needs is inside himself. There's no room for anyone else inside. Leonora and Little Frank are no longer players. His feelings exceed every-thing."

Senior says, "I don't understand that word you used, au-tonomy."

Mission Control [*in despair*]: "I hope he doesn't become a writer. I hope he leaves some room for his mother and father at least. But what's the point of hoping?"

Senior, still looking away, says, "You going to tell me, Tommy, what that word means? Or don't I have to know?" But the son, still looking at the floor, is gone: "He's gripped by the buffoon-ery of an emotion which exceeds his situation. Which exceeds all situations. He's the buffoon of sadness, remembering the livery of his nakedness. Once a year, he tries to resuscitate the dead art of the wheelbarrow, but he can't, because he doesn't want to repeat himself. On the porch, in summer, alone, he's not lonely. He's searching in the quicksand of himself for a new artistic ve-hicle. He's sucked down. He wants to be sucked down."

"Ann, what's he talking about?"

"I think our dear son is writing. I think he's sucked down."

Mission Control, a petite woman, comes into the kitchen. Senior stands. They embrace, then leave, holding hands. Junior remains seated: eyes wide; glazed over; corners of his mouth pulled down.

Alone, junior says, "The maximum happiness is to be in love with your unhappiness." He stands. He sits. Still alone, junior says, "He's deeply grateful for the gift of autonomy." He stands. He sits. He stands.

2 · A Fundamental Terror

Barely four days after the death of the distinguished American Wittgensteinian, BF Norman, his lover and literary executor—in a furious rummage among boxes of unpublished manuscripts— discovered several letters written by Norman which he, Gianni Morendo, the lover, promptly submitted to the *Wittgenstein Society Quarterly*. They appeared with a full-page photo of Norman at seventy-six; taken a week before his suicide; still oozing his fabled sensuality. The editors of *WSQ* had rushed headlong into print, knowing that Norman's enemies would seize the occasion to mount a vicious assault upon his posthumous philosophical authority. Over the objection of Sidra Singh, sole female member of the board, the editors decided to publish "only because" (as they wrote in a headnote to the letters) they were convinced that Norman's "striking evocation of a man unknown to the world," a man named Lucchesi, offered "poignant testimony" of Wittgenstein's "deepest humanity." LW's worst fear, they concluded, was ungrounded. His dark "forest of remarks" did, after all, "both engage and improve" the life of an ordinary man.

· · ·

May 19

Dear Wilhelm

After the traditional game of touch football, a stranger in his mid-forties, who introduced himself as Thomas Lucchesi, stood before me in a torrent of intensity and explained that the way we had spent the afternoon was so vile that we ought not to live, or at least he ought not to live, that nothing is tolerable except producing great works, which he could not produce, though he had tried, or enjoying those of others, but that he had seen all the great paintings, listened to all the great music, read all the great literature, and therefore was no longer capable of "orgasmic enjoyment," therefore etcetera. I suggested that he might cease seeking substitutes for sex and he responded in an absolutely dead tone: "Sex." The force with which the man spoke nearly knocked me down. I felt trivial; I *was* trivial. I also felt, and do feel, depressed, not only because of Mr. Lucchesi's painful (and oddly thrilling) scorn, but because I know that you continue to see Charles, though I've broken it off with Jennifer.

I suspect, by the way, that "Thomas Lucchesi" is a pseudonym.

· · ·

Jennifer darling

Today, a powerfully built man named Lucchesi, who exudes
sadness—he is one of the many mad amateurs attracted by our
annual meetings of mad Wittgensteinians—approached to in-
form me that our touch football games desecrated LW's memory. That we ought to invent a game; call it Wittgenstein; or call
it Game; so that all who play and all who spectate will be unavoidably aware of the purely conventional, site-specific func-
tion of the players within the rule-driven context of the game
itself. As he insanely put it, the players "above all must be re-
lentlessly aware of themselves as grammatical functions, even
while they play, who signify, in themselves, nothing at all." I
suggested to Mr. Sadness that when we play we like to throw
ourselves in whole hog. Forget everything, including LW's idea
of the language-game. That all the fun lies in forgetting oneself.
He said, "Only in death. In death do I trust." At which point I
recalled that when LW was told that he had but a day or two to
live, he said "Good." I recalled this but did not pass it on to Mr.
Lucchesi.

• • •

Gianni *Mio!*

Of course I do not "see" Vittoz and trust that you have "relin-
quished" Virog. Virog is so *rough*. Let the sex-game end. Please.
We are each other's Apostle, are we not?

95

An amateur philosopher, Thomas Lucchesi, who calls himself a writer, has been fairly lecturing me during the conference about my loyalty to LW. Says a Wittgensteinian who does not suffer ceaselessly is a fraud. Says I do not suffer, as is *indicated by my prose style*. I could not keep my eyes off him last night at the recital. Not what you think. He said, quite apropos of nothing that I could discern: "although I cannot give affection, I have a great need for it." Was this a perverse pass? Did he believe that I'd not recognize his quotation from the Master? Did he care? He announced to all at the conclusion of the panel on "Intention" that LW had fled from the "fundamental terror" within which the intentional act was embedded. He said, "To be human is to experience the perpetual pain of unrealizable intention. Because to be human means to want to be *someone else*. Because we, in ourselves, are empty. Only someone else is real. Does a lion desire to be another lion? Desiring that one's mane, the other's roar?" We were silenced.

Sidra sends best wishes. You do recall Sidra? The one who thinks that she can edit my style toward what she calls a pungent lucidity. At present, she says, I'm merely lucid. She gives me pain you know where.

• • •

May 22

Gianni! Gianni!

I neglected to tell you what I *saw* in Mr. Lucchesi at the recital. Keep in mind that we were sitting in the first row of the balcony. He did not lean forward. The jaw did not drop open, however slightly. The eyes did not glaze or bulge. None of the usual signs of transport, except the sadness was keener, the demeanor ghostlier. He was not *there*. After, I said to him, I gather that you are taken by Bryn Terfel. He said, I wanted to fling myself down on the stage. I said, assuming, of course, that he was not speaking literally, Quite a tribute to such a towering vocal genius! Such a volcano! He said, Fling myself down and kill myself. I said, But you would land in the middle of the orchestra and kill an innocent or two, along with yourself. Or worse, he said. I live and they die by breaking my fall. I said, You wish to die because you cannot be Mr. Terfel? He said, Apparently. I said, Perhaps you are misled. Recall what LW said: Our desires often conceal from us what we desire. He said, Yes, but not in my case.

I fear that Mr. Lucchesi may be darkly gifted. Sidra wants to lunch with me to discuss LW on interiority. According to Wilhelm, Sidra's capacity to bore is "unto an unlubricated dildo." Yes, her boredom penetrates, but in your absence, I shall submit. Wilhelm is dirty; simply dirty; fear him not.

· · ·

May 23

Dear Charles

You are right. Sidra is, *in principle,* a one-night stand. To be perfectly frank, in my case, a two-night stand, because this old philosopher who'd rather be in Rome is slow to arouse and Sidra is *so* unimaginative. On the antepenultimate night of the conference, I gave the plenary address, of course, and afterwards my seventy-fifth was celebrated. Quite a bash, dear one, with one exception. A man named Lucchesi, who's been *at* me the entire time, said that my lecture was very bad—that what I ought to do is say what *I* think, not discuss what LW thought, who talked only of his own thoughts, "nonstop." He said, Don't worry. You'll never understand Wittgenstein. I said, Thank you. He said, It's never too late to change, and then wished me a happy birthday.

I am in need of consolation. The plane ride is but an hour and I wish you would consider it.

• • •

June 7

Dear Gianni

Forgive my long and unforgivable silence. I have found some solace here in a cabin, deeply isolated, forty miles north of the conference center. Twenty miles off the nearest paved road. The conference is two weeks behind me now and in solitude I scribble notes on a personal name, yours, Gianni Morendo, trying my best to recover a sense of worth after the destruction visited upon me by Thomas Lucchesi. A destruction for which I can only be grateful, bringing me as it does to a view, however dim, of personal authenticity, at long last, in my seventy-fifth year. I have, as you know, well-earned my considerable international status as foremost commentator on the *Philosophical Investigations*. On the last night of the conference, without reason, and against my wishes, perhaps I just needed to undo myself *all the way down,* I spoke privately and at length with Lucchesi in my rooms. The subject, section 40 of the *Investigations,* a passage I know by heart in several languages and could explain to a child. Lucchesi made cunning reference to it (I say in retrospect) and I proceeded to quote the relevant portion: "the word 'meaning' is being used illicitly if it is used to signify the thing that 'corresponds' to the word. That is to confound the meaning of a name with the bearer of the name. When Mr. NN dies one says that the bearer of the name dies, not that the meaning dies. And it would be nonsensical to say that, for if the name ceased to have meaning it would make no sense to say 'Mr. NN is dead.'" I commented: "The meaning is indestructible, though we, the name-bearers, are not." He said, "Obviously. But who is Mr. NN?" I said, "Of course, LW deploys initials here. Name Name." "And who is *that,*" Lucchesi asked? "Precisely no one," I replied, "and anyone. Anyone who has a name. In other words, everyone. A general truth about personal names was reached by LW in section 40." Lucchesi said, "Precisely shit. LW fought general truths and theories. They are shit. But in section 40 he beshits himself. He, the Emperor of Particularity-in-Context, is doing precisely in section 40 the philosophy he would destroy." I said, "And what would you, sir?" He said, "I suggest that NN is the worst abomination possible for Wittgenstein. Why the initials of the word 'name'? Because the word 'name' is the name of an actual name, like David Pinsent,

99

his first lover, or Francis Skinner, his second. Kind and beautiful young men who died on him young and left him in despair. He sought maximum distance from those personal names, and from his endless personal pain. Hence NN, a pitiful, self-protective joke. He should have said DP or FS. He should have said DP and FS are dead, but their meaning in my pain lives, is indestructible in my pain, where they live." I said, "But that's not philosophy, is it?" Lucchesi replied, with contempt, "Which he didn't want to do, anyway. He was always threatening to leave philosophy. Because he wanted to honor the lives of real people. He wanted to help. He hated philosophy, but not enough. He wanted to say, David, Francis, come back to me. He wanted the greatest thing in the world: the warmth of a moist body, a kind and beautiful body. Beautiful *because* kind."

I saw that he was right and that I could not ever again do fundamental work in philosophy. I felt that my life-long impulse was shattered, like a wave against a breakwater, and I became filled with utter despair and needed to turn to you for consolation. But you were, so I thought, secretly occupied with Virog. So I took to casual philandering, and that has increased my despair. Lucchesi has persuaded me that what wanted doing was too difficult for me. Nevertheless, since his onslaught I have tried, the past two weeks, to do it. I have tried to do something helpful, and most unphilosophical, for myself. Thus I have written your name in my notebook a thousand times. An actual thousand. I have tried to describe you in your unique irregularity, your irreplaceable irregularity of being, but my words speak only the lies of regularity and I am desperate.

I asked Lucchesi what he was working on. He said, "An experimental fiction, of leviathanical proportions, about a man who would grasp the secret meaning of *Moby-Dick:* a man who becomes the mad Ahab of reading, who needs to strike through the artificial body of Melville's behemothian book, its mere seductive language, to the soul of it all, the univocal, insidious, backstabbing, deep significance, lurking in no single sentence of Melville's, not one! but embracing and informing them all." Then I told him that his criticisms of LW show that he was helped by LW to a discovery of a fierce and wonderful decency in himself, *you're* not empty, you're real, I said, but his work in progress tells us that he, like LW, and for a similar reason, is in process of self-beshitment and no doubt total insanity. For the first time since we'd met, he smiled, and then he left.

• • •

The letters of BF Norman published in *WSQ* were, in fact, as Mr. Morendo knew all along, never mailed. Clara Vittoz, chemist, was Norman's closest friend at Princeton; Virog is Paul Virog, the great Hungarian literary theorist. Wilhelm, Charles, and Jennifer have yet to be identified.

Gianni Morendo and Sidra Singh are now married and at work on Norman's official biography, which they refer to at philosophical conventions as "a cautionary narrative for our times." When last contacted, they declared no interest in Wilhelm, Charles, and Jennifer, whom they believe to be "banal, albeit vindictive fictions," and declined to interview "so-called" Thomas Lucchesi, whom (real or not) they are certain is Norman's greatest invention: "BF's technique of exposing himself to himself, and perhaps confronting, at the end, the horror of his pathetic emptiness," said Gianni Morendo, with the (typically) tacit approval of Sidra Singh.

Not being a reader of scholarly quarterlies, Thomas Lucchesi, who has long borne an uneasy relationship to his name, and who properly despairs of a place in literary history, never learned of the tiny but permanent place he'd won in the history of modern philosophy.

3 · The Logic of Love

Lucchesi aloft—inside the First Class cabin of an Alitalia 747 as it floats out, curving gently north by northeast over the coast of Newfoundland, bound for Rome. On the great wing, a word: BACI. Over the intercom, a voice, throaty and suggestive. He'll have eight more hours to decide: Was Wittgenstein kin or alien? He enjoys the partial rhyme. Oddly, enjoys this flight attendant too, now on her way, coming steadily toward him. Her animation. The terrible flood of her smile. The flood! Fondles his Wittgensteinian life-preservers: the *Tractatus,* the *Investigations,* the *Tractatus.*

There once was a man who was confused about his relations to bodies other than his own; possibly to his own as well. Who appeared to require sustained intimate contact with his mental processes and nothing else. Who attempted to become a philosopher (*writer!*) before becoming human. Then changed his mind, after becoming a famous philosopher (*unknown writer!*). He changed his mind, but was it too late? Whose grave is this, he asked? *Mine?!* I'll change!!! Lucchesi would become human, he would look into it, but after sixty-five? When in Rome, he'll call on the Pope. Wittgenstein is dead; he died.

She brings the beverage cart to a halt and says, the intercom voice says, "May I do something for you? May I pour your etcetera?" Lucchesi, all crimson, looks up from the *Tractatus*. She looks down at the book and reads aloud from decimal 5.101: "'If *p* then *q*.'" She says, "If *me* [pauses] then *you?* Would you like to sip?" For a full two seconds, Lucchesi feels this gigantic plane flip violently, end over end. In a cold sweat, from memory, he quotes the *Tractatus*, 1.1: "'The world is the totality of facts, not things.'" She says, "Ah!" He says, "Come again?" She says, "Ahhhhhh." He says, "Me and you are not facts; we're things." She says, "I rather enjoy my thing. Do you enjoy yours?" Through the mask of obliviousness, he continues, "A fact is a necessary relationship. Facts, not things, in logical space are the world. [*Crosses legs. Hugs himself.*] We, you and me . . . me and you . . . from the epistemological . . . in the epistemological . . ." With a brightening glance, she says, "Certainly! The epistemological! Even the ontological!" He says, "We, you and me, exist

103

in the pigsty of real space and time, not in logical space. Our relationship cannot be necessary. Logically speaking. Therefore, we are not in the world. Logically speaking." She says, "I can dig it." He says, "No. You do not understand, though you may indeed dig it. The real world is a charnel house of failed causalities." She says, "Surprises. We are surprised constantly by the real world." He says, "The real world, like me and you, is unnecessary and unknowable from the logical point of view, which is my point of view. On the other hand, 'If p then q' is rigorous; it is unavoidable; it is smooth; it is white; it is cold; it is clean clean clean! Can you visualize the ice caps?" She says, "Which one?" He says, "I speak metaphorically." She says, "Publicly?" He says, "My God." She says, "Visualize this: Later, lights off, and I'm drinking your drink, pouring it down my throat, then down yours, unavoidably and rigorously. Can you possibly wait?" She moves on down the aisle. He says, "Wait a minute! Ruth! The sentence 'If p then q' is a word picture of hypothetical fact. Don't you see? Pictorial structure and the structure of fact are one and the same. No logical world outside the word picture ('If p then q'), none whatsoever! You and me are not in the word picture ('If p then q'). Pouring into the mouth, down the throat, whether yours or mine, is not in the picture ('If p then q'). Come back! Ruth! Only logico-pictorial form is in the picture, it *is* the picture, and logico-pictorial form is also what the picture represents. The word picture reaches out to the logical world and the logical world cries, 'Darling!' No gap! Mirrors upon mirrors! Don't you just love it? The pouring and the sipping and the horniness are not in the word picture ('If p then q'). Oh, Ruth!" She turns and says, "I don't love it." He says, "We are among the damned, the rough contingencies, the accidents of blood that drift in the filth of time. We're doomed." She turns again, smiles, and says: "Did you just write something? Because people don't talk that way. Especially people who are doomed. I don't believe that you're doomed." She laughs and comes back to him. She whispers, "Words turn you on? The filth of time? I'm afraid that, on this flight, Mr. Lucchesi, we have no dirty pictures, though maybe later I'll relieve you of your point of view. Because you do need to be relieved, Mr. Lucchesi."

He winces inwardly, where she can't see, at the pronunciation of his name. To what she cannot see, she cannot respond. He might as well be a chair. She leaves. Lou-chee-zee. Variant number 3 out of 9. Sounding like dialect Italian for, She kills him. Or was it, He kills her? Wittgenstein had much to say about names in the *Investigations*, reassuring and disturbing at the same time. A mystery that Lucchesi had not yet been able to solve. He thought that those meditations on names might even be the secret key to Wittgenstein's long twilight struggle to save himself from the ice world. Which one, she'd asked? Arctic? Antarctic? Was she some kind of comedian in disguise? He'll follow the thread of notes on names, later. Now he'll enjoy his astonishing good fortune, thanks to the shelling of the Italian Adriatic coast, the left wing riots in Milan and Rome, the car bombs in Paris, the endless hostage crisis in London (at the Old Vic!), and now these arrogant international carriers operating in the European Theater of this blood contagion of the Balkans all crying bankruptcy, with Alitalia leading the plunge. One of its craft destroyed by an errant NATO missile: 465 corpses later and here he is, this impoverished writer, Thomas Lucchesi, in First Class, with two seats for the peacetime price of high season coach fare for one. Lucchesi, sole passenger in First Class, making speeches about Wittgenstein to a sexy flight attendant in her late forties. Next to him, his intimates: notebook, legal pads, pencils, pens, texts by and about Wittgenstein, a copy of his latest novel (published by an obscure art press, at his expense, in an edition of 87), and, later, with the arm rest up, and his intimates locked safely away in his carry-on, a bed, with it up *and Ruth straddling him with it up,* 36,000 feet over the Irish Sea. How many air nautical miles would they cover from connection to orgasm? A new measure of manhood. The thought stirs in his crotch, somewhat, then depresses him, more than somewhat. In his picture, for sometime now, no love-making.

Of course, Wittgenstein knew. He knew everything, this Wittgenstein. Knew that love-making displays no logico-pictorial form, could not be part of the picture ('If p then q'), ever, and so he tried to become human. He sought love outside the picture? He dared to go outside. Lucchesi feels inadequate to the task. Where does anyone find the courage to go outside? Then the staying-power to stay human? And would it have been worthwhile after all? He'd prefer to know in advance, before opening the door.

On his deathbed, from within his deepest humanity, of this Lucchesi is convinced, Wittgenstein told John Maynard Keynes that he would have liked to have composed a philosophical work consisting entirely of jokes. Keynes asked why he hadn't. Wittgenstein replied, "Sadly, I don't have a sense of humor." And just before the last blackout: "Tell them I've had a wonderful life." Lucchesi feels that it would be the greatest happiness, an incontestable triumph over the vast negativity of life, to die talking that way. If only God would grant him in his last hours some rationality, *if only I believed in God,* what he'd do is quote Wittgenstein's deathbed gems to those gathered around him, but wouldn't mention that he was quoting. In his own writing, in his so-called "own," he'd quoted without mentioning it and heard the dead men he'd quoted say, "Brother." Say, "This is what we do. Welcome home, brother." Lucchesi hears himself think "those gathered around" and can't imagine a group of actual people at his bedside, with names and familiar faces to go with the names, and he winces again, this time visibly, dramatically, as she walks back toward him.

She stops. She whispers in her husky way, "It's going to turn out well." He looks up, still in pain, and says to her utter incomprehension, "Tell *them*. Tell *them*. He was totally confident that there would be at the end those who would care and who would want to remember his words. And would remember. Because they loved him. This is why he said 'wonderful.' Because he knew that the love was out there. For him." She leans over and says, "It'll turn out happily, Thomas. You'll see," then moves on. Lucchesi says, too quietly, he swallows the words, "Come back, Ruth." But she doesn't hear his plea.

Left to himself, to brood on the absurdity: an Alitalia flight attendant who cannot properly pronounce an Italian surname. In the global village, we become neighbors with those who cannot pronounce our names, and we cannot pronounce theirs. Globalization? Ceaseless aural pollution. This Ruth Cohn. Where was she from? He can't say. Co-hen or Cone? One of the two. He had learned the distinction in what used to be called America. But "Lucchesi" they had never gotten right, not even in his so-called home town, where they're supposed to get you right, and now they get it wrong on an Italian airliner. When they mispronounce you in your homeland, can you be at home? When there is a difference of pronunciation even among members of your extended family, do you belong to a family? Makes a phonetic list in his notebook of the mispronunciations that he's heard of his surname in America: Luck-easy; Lou-seize-ee; Lou-chee-zee; Lou-keys-ee (one of his cousins!); Lou-cheese-eye; Lou-seize-eye; Lou-keys-eye; Lou-casy (one of his uncles!); Lou-kay-zee (*yes!*). Why does he feel, why should he feel, what is the word? *Wounded? Sad?* Each time they get it wrong. *Alone?* "Lucchesi": plural; masculine; from Lucca, *provincia di Toscana,* where he was not from. *Absurd.* His grandparents (all four) were born in Naples. Was there anything right about his name? Had he ever, truly, felt a rightness about it, in itself, to himself? Is he plural? If so, would that be good or bad?

Of this he is certain: he is not a chair. Wittgenstein had used the word "chair" in the *Investigations* as an example of a name, and that's where he believes that Wittgenstein got it wrong. Because can a chair care about its name? Can a chair feel alone and alien because its name is mispronounced? If it has them, a chair doesn't display its feelings. If it displays its feelings, we can't read them, not being natives of chair culture. Ludwig the whimsical. How a chair gestures in frustration, grimaces, yells: we're closed out. Why did LW sometimes think of a person's name as if it were no different than "chair"? In the humane period of the *Investigations,* when he escaped from the ice field of his mind, maybe he hadn't, because he was also Ludwig the terrible, who refused to consider, from the inside point of view, how a human feels about its name, in the privacy of its inside, particularly when the pronunciation is butchered. LW thought of private feelings, the invisible ones to all who stand outside, and all except you stand outside, in the same way that he thought of a chair's. No existence in human culture. We can't play with them in the language-games of life. You can't speak of your private feelings, because if you do, they're no longer private and invisible. And never, never speak of them silently to yourself, because if you do, you betray your secrecy, though only you will know. Language? The uncatchable thief of privacy. *Am I a chair? Even to myself? Son of a bitch!*

Lucchesi clings stubbornly to the singular secret of himself.

The best part of me, as he thought, the undisplayable and impregnable citadel of my true self, better than any precious bodily fluids, which have on distant occasions been displayed. *Wittgenstein on the names of people ignores the inner sanctum, the unspeakable and incorruptible humanness of the name-bearer. Wittgenstein flees the human, homesick for the ice.* For a man like Thomas Lucchesi, who never thought of himself as "like" anybody, who loved to think inside the refrigerator of the *Tractatus,* this "subversive insight" (as he thought of it) into the *Investigations* should have been heartening. No change, after all, from early to late Wittgenstein. *Ruth.* Into his meditation she comes, *Ruth,* he can't say why. *Ruth. Her animation; her animal.* Thickening (*some*), in the crotch. Would like to, with her, *here.* To be a snow man no more. He would find the torrid zone in the *Investigations,* as if Wittgenstein's desperate, long leap into the human world would make his own possible. Make what possible? *My erection?* He wanted Wittgenstein himself to be his bridge; a man of ice, as he thought of himself, walking over a bridge built by the ice man of all ice men. Welcome to the Real. Pouring and sipping permitted.

He forages like a starved raccoon through the main points of Wittgenstein's meditations on names. Writes them into his notebook with piquant commentary. He'll discuss his revelations with Ruth. When? As a preface to the straddling. Lucchesi laughs loud, a little wildly. Just a little. She returns. Says, "Can I be of assistance?" He says, "Yes. Bring me a viagra and tonic." She's paralyzed. She did not expect such talk from this man. He says, "Look at this," and begins to read from his notes and remarks on the *Investigations*. "Never confound the meaning of a name with the bearer of a name. [*She touches his neck.*] Please, Ruth, give me a little time. A name corresponds with a bearer, but the meaning does not. Ruth. Hear me out. The bearer dies; the meaning is indestructible. The meaning of the meaning of a name, therefore, becomes exceptionally vivid after the death of the bearer of the name. Wittgenstein is dead, but 'Wittgenstein' lives! Name-use is the fuel of immortality. Use grants life after death. When we don't say the names, we become the cruel gods who cut off the fuel supply. We disuse to assassinate." She says, "You're warm." He says, "Poor Melville. Even before his death, he was dead in Manhattan, because they didn't say his name. His name languished in limbo, yearning for utterance. Then, long after his bodily demise, they started again. The scholars first. Melville, Melville, they said. Arise! And he arose again." She says, "Soon. You too will rise. Soon." He says, "To say the name is to make its meaning alive, though the bearer is dead. Think of this: if all the human bearers die but one, then language still lives and all the dead bearers may return in the body of their names-in-use, in the game of language, spoken by the last man in silent and imaginary conversations with all the dead. My dear Ruth, the actual death of a man is incidental to his true life in culture and history. We achieve transcendence of the body: Wittgenstein's great theme! We are welcomed into our home, the living language; in the actual mouths of the living. We're the noise of many tongues, on the tongue."

Ruth says, "Yes. The tongue. But we already know this, don't we? This is what we do. Is this news?" And Lucchesi responds, "And that is precisely Wittgenstein's point about philosophy's authentic mission. The people already know, like you, because they *do*. They act. Ruth, you are a true Wittgensteinian; you have surpassed philosophy. But the philosophers! If only he can get it through their stupid thick skulls, no more philosophy!" Ruth says, "Until tonight I never saw or heard the name of this Wittgenstein." Lucchesi says, "Sit here." Puts away his things. Says, "The demonstrative 'this' [*touches her face*] can never be without a bearer, according to [*her thigh*] Wittgenstein. By saying 'this Wittgenstein' you bring him beside us. You make him present." Ruth says, "I don't go in for threesomes. Melville? I saw his name once at Barnes & Noble in Beijing, but never heard it said until tonight." Lucchesi says, "You just said it. Melville is here. You say Lou-chee-zee, some say Lou-seize-ee, and this is perhaps not the pollution of my life that I have long thought it to be. Perhaps the cacophony of all the ways that my name may be said is the purest oxygen. I leave the airless nowhere of my inner sanctum. I inhabit different mouths and circulate in and among the living. [*She touches his face.*] In my lifetime I circulate, but after death, who knows? Wittgenstein said, 'Tell them I've had a wonderful life.' The wonder was that he knew in advance that he'd circulate after death. Now, Ruth, I circulate. Now. This [*touch-*

ing her breast] is not nothing. This is what I know: they give me plural life, the mouths of the living. [*He kisses her.*] What does my invisible (to you) inside point of view, on how I feel invisibly (to you) about my name, or about anything else, give me except the pain of isolation?" Ruth says, "I don't think you want that, is what you're telling me, but who does?" Lucchesi answers, "Some of us cultivate our secrecy in the search for death-in-life. Wittgenstein saw in the *Investigations* that to be human you must circulate in and through the mouths—" She says, "On the tongue." He says, "Yes. Of course. The tongue. Speaking in conversations of you, to you, at you, for you, in gossip against you—" She says, "In you." He says, "That too. In you. And this is your true life. When you don't circulate, what are you? [*She kisses him.*] We are social or we are chairs."

Ruth asks, "Have you been social, sweetheart?" Lucchesi answers, "I fear not." She asks, "Was Wittgenstein? I mean the person who walked around. Not the one who wrote. Forget about the man who wrote." Lucchesi says, "After the death of David Pinsent, Wittgenstein wrote of him, in a letter, as 'my first and my only friend.' They strolled, hand in hand, in the country, chatting of mathematical logic. They sailed together, silent on a fjord in Norway." Ruth says, "Ludwig and Pinescent." Lucchesi says, "Tremendous point, darling. How do we pronounce his name? Where is the accent, for example? Perhaps Ludwig actually became playful on those walks and called him Pinescent, with his head on sweet David's shoulder, inhaling his musk. The pinescent! And now David, unspoken of all these years, Ruth. He's here." She says, "Thomas. Are you happy? May I touch your secrecy?" [*Unzips his fly.*] He says, "If *David* then *Ludwig?*" [*Puts her hand in.*] She says, "Sounds logical." He says, "Say it again. Say Lou-chee-zee." She says, "Wait a minute." Leaves. Lights go down. In the dark, she comes to him, with the arm rest up.

When he comes to consciousness, Ruth and an actual Italian, the flight engineer, are standing over him. The flight engineer is saying, "He have big hard attack?" Lucchesi smiles and says, "No. Chronic vertigo." Ruth says, "Hard attack." Lucchesi says, "Tell him that I'm not dying, Ruth." Ruth says, "He's dying, but not now."

They cannot land in Italy. Terrorism etcetera. They must fly to another country. Where? Unclear. They will disembark into an unknown tongue and, with difficulty, they will circulate. Or maybe not. The craft is vibrating, maybe dangerously. Over the intercom, from the flight deck, a shout: "*O Dio!*"

Alone. Ruth and Thomas. He is exhausted. He never knew that he wanted a woman like her. Thinks: Ruth has force. Speaks:

"Did I?"

"We. Yes."

"I did?!"

"Yes. We."

"I'm a writer, you know."

"Clearly."

"Did I actually?"

114

"Say we."

"Over the Irish Sea?"

"The turbulence!"

"We might die. We might be doomed."

"We're aloft."

"We. We were turbulent together!"

"Yes."

"Together!"

"In me, like a great river, you circulate."

Postscript to "The Logic of Love"

I will say, because desire and truth do equally require it, that Jody McAuliffe has given me literary advice worthy of Ezra Pound. And more—this the greatest gift—that her compassion for my trials, on and off the page, has been, and is, the miracle of my life.

Frank Lentricchia is the Katherine Everett Gilbert Professor of
Literature at Duke University. He is the author of numerous critical
books and novels, including *The Music of the Inferno* (1999), *Johnny
Critelli and The Knifemen: Two Novels* (1996), *Modernist Quartet* (1994),
The Edge of Night: A Confession (1994), *Ariel and the Police: Michel
Foucault, William James, Wallace Stevens* (1988), *Criticism and Social
Change* (1983), *After the New Criticism* (1980), *Robert Frost: A
Bibliography, 1913–1974* (1976), *Robert Frost: Modern Poetics and
the Landscapes of Self* (1975), *The Gaiety of Language: An Essay on the
Radical Poetics of W. B. Yeats and Wallace Stevens* (1968). He is also the
editor of *Introducing Don DeLillo* (1991), *New Essays on White Noise*
(1991), and, with Thomas McLaughlin, *Critical Terms for Literary Study*
(1990, second ed., 1995).

Library of Congress Cataloging-in-Publication Data
Lentricchia, Frank.
Lucchesi and the whale / Frank Lentricchia.
p.   cm. — (Post-contemporary interventions)
ISBN 0-8223-2654-X (cloth : alk. paper)
1. Melville, Herman, 1819–1891—Appreciation—Fiction.   2. Fiction—
Authorship—Fiction.   3. College teachers—Fiction.   4. Middle
West—Fiction.   5. Friendship—Fiction.   6. Grief— Fiction.   I. Title.
II. Series.
PS3562.E4937 L83 2001   813'.54—dc21   00-063844